THE DEVIL'S PEACEMAKER

From the Wild West comes the renegade manhunter, Vinton Stroud, carrying an ornate gun known as the Devil's Peacemaker. Hired by a ruthless cattle-baron, the killer leaves a trail of bullets, blood and bodies. Also riding into Holliday is Jim Sutter, looking to leave his old job of manhunting behind. However, having come to the aid of a rancher's beautiful daughter, he finds himself next on the list of the vicious killer, and embroiled in a life-or-death struggle . . .

Books by Lance Howard
in the Linford Western Library:

THE COMANCHE'S GHOST
THE WEST WITCH
THE GALLOWS GHOST
THE WIDOW MAKER
GUNS OF THE PAST
PALOMITA
THE LAST DRAW
THE DEADLY DOVES
WANTED

LANCE HOWARD

THE DEVIL'S PEACEMAKER

Complete and Unabridged

LINFORD
Leicester

First published in Great Britain in 2000 by
Robert Hale Limited
London

First Linford Edition
published 2002
by arrangement with
Robert Hale Limited
London

The moral right of the author
has been asserted

British Library CIP Data

Howard, Lance
   The Devil's Peacemaker.—Large print ed.—
Linford western library
1. Western stories
2. Large type books
I. Title
823.9'14 [F]

ISBN 0–7089–9766–X

Published by
F. A. Thorpe (Publishing)
Anstey, Leicestershire

Set by Words & Graphics Ltd.
Anstey, Leicestershire
Printed and bound in Great Britain by
T. J. International Ltd., Padstow, Cornwall

This book is printed on acid-free paper

1

Lo! Death has reared himself
  a throne
In a strange city lying alone
Far down within the dim West
Where the good and the bad and
  the worst and the best
Have gone to their eternal rest.
                    Edgar Allan Poe
              The City in the Sea

The ranch-house door burst inward with a shuddering crash and Cyrus Pendelton knew death had come a-calling. The force of the kick splintered the frame around the latch and caused the door to rebound from the wall, only to be stopped dead by a black-gloved hand that caught its edge.

If such a thing as death personified existed it stood there in the doorway. Backlit by splashes of moonlight, the form shimmered like an avenging black demon in the shape of a man. The figure pushed the door inward and surveyed the interior of the house, which was lit by a single kerosene lamp sitting on a table and flickering firelight that capered like giggling amber spectres on the rough-hewn walls. A cool October wind brought in the scents of old leather, sweat and whiskey; the aroma of death.

The pipe Cyrus had been nursing dropped from his lips; the clatter it made striking the floorboards might as well have had the snapping thunder of a gunshot, the way it braced his nerves.

'What the tarnation do you want, Mister?' he demanded in a voice that didn't come out half as forceful as he intended.

The figure took a couple of inward steps. Each bootfall on the puncheon floorboards banged hollow like a coffin lid dropping shut. 'You Cyrus Pendelton?' Fire and lantern light washed over a pale face that held no trace of compassion or mercy — the face of a killer, Cyrus thought. A killer as loco as a coyote on the foam.

'Yeah, I'm him . . . ' The words came out almost a whisper and Cyrus wasn't proud of it. He had never backed down to any man or beast in near to seventy years, but something about this fella plain boogered him.

The man took another step, spurs jangling on scuffed black boots, black duster swishing. 'Reckon we got business . . . *outside*.'

Cyrus scrutinized the man more closely and was damned if he could pick out a single redeeming feature. There might have been something once, a kind of dark nobility that lay just out of glimpse, but if it had indeed been there it was gone now, devoured by a demon of cold black duty. Killing was this fella's job, his passion. Cyrus saw it in the man's dark eyes, in every chiselled line of his stony face, in the turn of thin cruel lips nearly hidden by a soup-strainer mustache.

The man peeled hide gloves from his hands and shoved them into his duster, then removed his Stetson and ran a hand over slicked-back, black hair parted in the middle. 'You best make it easy on yourself, old man. This won't take long — if'n I'm in a merciful mood.'

'I got no business with you,' Cyrus said, mustering a measure of defiance. He wouldn't have called it courage, no, not that; stubbornness, more like, a last spark of the man he had been before the years had worn away his toughness, before the West had taken the last drops of whatever made his lifeblood piss and vinegar and turned it into diluted rotgut. The man he had been before Jesse passed on, leaving him to bring up a daughter by his lonesome and make ends meet on this ranch deep in the bowels of New Mex Territory.

'Beg to differ, sir. Mr Stark says he's got right due to this spread and I aim to enforce that claim.' The man swept his duster back to reveal a Peacemaker resting in a tooled leather holster. It was the biggest galldamn piece Cyrus recollected laying eyes on, black except for its handle, which was fashioned out of yellowed ivory carved with the relief of a ram's head.

He recognized this man, now, by reputation only, but that was enough.

'Stroud . . . ' Cyrus whispered, the sound dying on his lips.

A grim light danced in the man's black eyes. 'Reckon you heard of me.'

'I heard of you. And you ain't welcome in my home. Stark ain't neither.' Cyrus wondered if the man could see him shaking. Now that he knew who this man was he thanked God Almighty Ruby was out tending to a sick horse in the stable and wouldn't — '

'Father?' A voice came from the doorway and the figure standing before him spun.

'What are you doin' here, Ruby?' His voice quivered and he felt his heart plunge. 'You're s'posed to be out tendin' that mount.'

Her gaze flicked from Stroud to Cyrus, growing hard, suspicious. 'I saw this fella ride up. He looked like two days of a blue norther.'

The man named Stroud turned back to Cyrus and his hand drifted to the handle of his Peacemaker. 'Don't make me take you 'fore I'm ready, Pendelton.' His voice came low, pregnant with threat.

'What's goin' on, Father?' A flame sparked in Ruby's hazel eyes; the venom she held in them as she peered at Stroud would have stopped a rattlesnake in its tracks. 'What's this fella want? What's he doin' in our home?'

Cyrus stood. His arms quivered as he gripped the chair; his legs shook as if he'd been in the saddle a week.

'This here fella's a gen-u-ine legend, Ruby.'

She shook her blonde head and he knew she would have none of it. 'Legend? Reckon I don't understand, nor do I care to.'

Cyrus knew she saw the man for what he was. Ruby was perceptive that way and likely even a mite tougher than he, when it came to standing up for herself. If he had instilled one positive thing in her that was it. A body needed the toughness out here. This land ate folks up and spat them to hell and back and if she were to go on without him and keep what was rightfully hers she would need that durability and a good measure more.

'Why don't you tell the filly who I am, old man?'

Cyrus ran his tongue over dry lips and shifted his gaze to his daughter. 'This man here is Vinton Stroud, a famous mankiller. Read about him in them dime novels. He's the deadliest shootist the West ever seen, if the claim of those books is right.'

'A murderer . . . ' Her voice went cold and something flickered in Stroud's black eyes — annoyance? That strange lost sense of nobility Cyrus thought he glimpsed?

Hell, maybe it was just plain meanness.

'Murderers have no sense of justice, ma'am.' Stroud's lips barely moved. The coldness in his tone matched hers. 'I do.'

'The hell you've got any sense of anything humanly decent, Mr Stroud!' Her voice snapped like a whip and she took a step towards him. 'You're no better than a common bandit robbing a stage. Get the hell out of here 'fore I put a load of shot in your britches or fetch the marshal.'

'Cussin' ain't right attractive on a filly, ma'am.' He said it with as much mockery in his flat tone as Cyrus ever heard. The mankiller had read his daughter, found the burr that would stick in her saddle. Ruby hated being told to be a woman.

'You're a waste of hide!' Anger sparkled in her hazel eyes. 'You got no right comin' in our home this way and you can just take your sorry britches on out again, 'fore I decide it's sportin' season on lowdown skunks!'

The only hint Stroud was perturbed was an almost unnoticeable deepening of the lines in his forehead. 'Beg to differ, ma'am. But I rightly expect no less from the likes of you and this land-grabber.'

Ruby's cheeks reddened. 'I ain't sayin' it again, Mr Stroud. Get out of our home. I don't give a wooden nickel 'bout your reputation or whatever reason you think you came here for. Get out 'fore I fill you full of holes.'

Cyrus knew she meant it. She was already eyeing the gunbelt that hung over a hard-backed chair and the Winchester resting on wall pegs.

'Oh, I'll leave, Miss Pendelton . . . soon as I finish what I came here to do.'

'What you came here to do?' She looked at Cyrus and he felt a cold wave wash over him.

'Rutherford Stark sent him, Ruby. Sent him to take what ain't his. He aims to kill me, I do believe.'

Stroud's expression darkened. 'I'll give you a sportin' chance, sir.' He nudged his head towards the gunbelt on the chair. 'Pick it up and strap it on. I'm callin' you out, Pendelton, in the name of justice. You are charged with stealin' horses from Mr Stark and refusin' to leave land rightly belongin' to him.'

'That's plumb loco!' Ruby yelled. 'He's seventy years old and sick. He ain't got a chance against the likes of you!' Ruby made a lunge for the gunbelt lying across the back of the chair, but Cyrus stepped in front of her, preventing the young woman from grabbing the Smith & Wesson in the holster. 'Let me go! He's loco. He'll kill you. I won't let him!'

Stroud let out a laugh. 'Much as I'm touched by this display of loyalty, ma'am, it don't change the outcome none. You and your father got some-thin' Mr Stark wants. I aim to bring that end about.'

'I don't give a horned owl's hoot what Mr Stark wants,' Ruby said through gritted teeth. 'He's a bastard and a crook as big as they grow 'em. Why don't you use your justice on him?'

For an instant something serious played in Stroud's eyes and Cyrus wondered if Rutherford Stark hadn't climbed onto a horse he couldn't ride. The look vanished and the shootist edged backward towards the door.

'You got two minutes, Pendelton. Best go out like a man. Don't make me come back in for you. I don't like it that way . . .'

'The hell with what you like!' Ruby yelled, breaking free of her father's grip. He saw fury in her eyes, but also something else: fear, the fear her father was about to be taken from her and she plain refused to let that happen. 'You can't fight him, Father. You ain't no gunslinger.'

'Got no choice, honey. He ain't gonna take what's ours without a fight.

I never backed down to no man, and I won't start with Rutherford Stark or the likes of him.'

The mankiller smiled the smile of a rattlesnake poised to strike. 'Two minutes, sir . . . ' Stroud backed out the door.

Cyrus made his voice firm. 'I gotta face him, Ruby. He ain't givin' me a choice and he'll kill us both if I don't.'

A tear slid from her eye and he couldn't remember having seen her cry since the day Jesse passed. 'He'll kill us anyway, Father. I see it in his eyes. He won't stop. Let me help. It's our only chance.'

Cyrus shook his head slowly and his leathery face took on a grim look. He pulled a watch from his trouser pocket, flipping back the carved metal cover of an iron horse and glanced at the hands. 'Time's up, honey. I best do what needs doin'.'

He turned and gathered the belt from the chair.

'No . . . ' Her hands went to her

mouth, trembling. Resignation poured into her eyes. 'Please don't go out there.'

He gave her a look as close to compassion and understanding as he was capable of mustering. He had never been particularly good at expressing his feelings to her. He'd raised her and tended to her needs, fashioned her into more a reflection of his ideals and feistiness than anything the highfalutin' folk would have considered womanly, but that was all he knew and he hoped to God Almighty he had done some right. God granted no second chances on things like that in this life. 'It'll be awright, Ruby. Get yourself some help. Find someone you can trust and go somewhere else with him. Let Stark have this land. It ain't worth your life.'

'The hell I will . . . ' she whispered, tears streaming down her face. 'The hell I will.'

Going to a small writing table, he opened a drawer, bringing out a box of Winchester shells and pocketing them.

He didn't want Ruby getting any ideas.

'Time's up, old man. I'm waitin' on ya.' The voice drifted through the door, an ill wind.

Cyrus glanced in that direction, back to his daughter. 'Hell, Ruby, maybe I ain't never told you but you're the only thing past your mother I ever gave a damn about. Don't let a man like that one out there take that from me.'

'Please . . . don't go out there. You know you can't beat him.'

Resolution tightened his face. 'I don't, he'll come in here and I'll have a whole lot more to lose than just my life.'

Turning, he went through the door. The night air slapped his face and he drew a steadying breath. He saw Stroud standing there, marbled black and alabaster with moonlight and shadow.

'Let's get this done, Mr Pendleton. I got more justice to dole out tonight.'

Cyrus gave a grim nod and strapped the gunbelt around his waist. Inside the house he heard Ruby sobbing. Or maybe it was the wind.

Cyrus took a final glance at the ranch house and at the other buildings, stable, outhouse and corral, and whispered a sombre goodbye. The accumulation of a man's life. What the hell was it really worth in the end?

His gaze went back to the house as Ruby stepped outside. By the look on her face she intended to stop this somehow, even if it meant her death.

Stroud must have noticed the same thing. 'Tell your daughter to not interfere, Mr Pendleton. I'll kill her just as easy as you please if'n she does.'

Cyrus looked at his daughter, a plea in his eyes. 'Please, Ruby, honour the last wish of an old man and don't do what's in your mind. I gotta go out knowin' you got a chance.'

She plainly didn't want to agree; he saw that. He knew her indomitable spirit and he knew she was part of him and maybe that was as comforting as anything he could have asked for. He had raised her right, raised her with honour and sturdiness and didn't have to regret it a lick. Jesse would have been proud.

She nodded reluctantly and more tears streamed down her face.

He turned back to Stroud, who was grinning like the Devil pulling a marker.

'When you're ready, Stroud . . . ' Cyrus's hand shook as it hovered over the Smith & Wesson. Christamighty, was the piece even loaded? Hell of a time to worry about that.

It didn't matter. Loaded or not, he was a dead man.

' 'Thy soul shall find itself alone', Mr Pendleton, 'mid dark thoughts of the grey tombstone — ' '

He saw the insanity wash over Stroud's eyes then, the lust for killing. The man vanished, the soul replaced by nothingness, the nothingness of corruption and perverted duty.

'You're loco . . . ' Cyrus whispered.

Stroud's smile drew darker. 'Edgar Allan Poe, Mr Pendelton. *Spirits of the*

Dead.' Stroud's hand moved. It swept downward towards the Peacemaker faster than anything Cyrus had ever seen and he tried to get his own quivering hand in motion. He barely reached the handle of his Smith & Wesson before Stroud's gun cleared leather and a thundering shot pounded in his ears.

For an instant he thought nothing had happened but sound. There was simply the reverberation of the shot, the billowing of blue smoke frosted with moonlight.

Then came pain, a fraction behind the tremendous kick of lead punching through his ribs. He felt bone splinter. Jolted backwards, he crumpled to the ground. Agony engulfed his chest and his quaking hand went to the gaping hole near his heart. Warm wetness ran over his fingers and flowed to the ground, mingling with dust. His watch slid from his pocket and he was vaguely aware of Stroud stooping close, picking it up and shoving it inside his duster.

Distantly he heard Ruby scream and through clouding vision saw her run towards him. She fell to his side, frantically clutched his frail frame to her breast, tears dripping from her face onto his. He gazed up at her and his lips moved, feebly trying to form words.

'I . . . love . . . you . . . ' There. He had said it. For the first time in his life he told her those words and now they were out and she knew.

'I never doubted it, Father. I never doubted it.' The words quivered with tears.

Pain.

So much goddamn pain.

Hell. It was fading now. Maybe he would be OK. Maybe the damage wasn't as . . .

★ ★ ★

Her father's eyelids fluttered shut and Ruby knew he was gone. Every emotion inside her burst free, overwhelming waves of loss and grief, and a sense that she was now totally and utterly alone. Anger welled, fury at the being in black who stood in the moonlight, gazing at his corrupt work.

She pulled him closer, kissing his forehead, shaking with the cascading rush of emotions in her heart. She stayed that way a very long time, heedless of the night and demon of a man standing a short distance away.

An eternity dragged by.

A shiver of coldness swept over her and she looked up at the sound of hoof-falls approaching.

The black figure sat poised in the saddle, peering down at her without sympathy or compassion.

'Bastard. Murderer.' Her lips trembled. Her voice came deadly low. 'I swear you'll pay for this with the last breath I take.'

'You got a week to clear off this property, ma'am. My employer claims right to this land.'

Defiance swarmed in her eyes. 'I won't be leavin' this land, Mr Stroud.

You can damn well count on that. It belongs to . . . us.'

Stroud let out a humourless laugh. It stopped abruptly and for a moment he seemed to change, eyelids fluttering. His hand went to his temple. Beads of sweat glittering with moonlight broke out on his forehead. Then he lowered his hand, as if whatever spell had taken him had passed. 'Beg to differ, ma'am. You'll be leavin' it — under your own power or in the back of a wagon.' He gripped the reins and pulled his horse's head up, ready to ride. 'Don't rightly matter to me which way you choose. Mr Stark granted you that option.' He reined around and gigged his horse into a gallop. Clods of dirt flew up and showered her body, but she didn't flinch, didn't take her gaze from the man who receded into the distance like a black ghost vanishing in the dawn.

He would pay. Somehow. Fire with fire. Whatever way it came about. She would never leave this land, she would never leave her father's years of work and memory. Stroud would have to kill her.

Unless she got him first.

Then her resolve trickled away and she wept to the cold moon for a very long time.

2

'Jim Sutter, you young, whippersnapper lawman wannabe!' shouted Marshal Frank Glover, as the young man came through the door of his office. The marshal jumped from his hard-backed chair and rushed over to greet the man doffing his Stetson.

Jim Sutter returned the expression. 'How the hell you been, you old lawdog? Ain't you retired yet?'

'End of this here year, son, end of this here year.' He pumped the younger man's hand, his creased face beatific. 'Been a coon's age. What in the Lord Almighty's fine name brings you to Holliday?'

Jim Sutter set his hat on a rack, and smoothed back his sandy-blond hair. Broad across the shoulders, he carried himself with a quiet confidence that usually came with more experienced men. Deep-blue eyes roving, he glanced around the sparsely furnished office to the rack holding a scatter-gun and Winchester, then on to the two jail cells — empty of customers — at the back, the scuffed and worn desk directly opposite the dust-coated window. Everything was just as he recollected it and it gave him a solid sense of comfort. He was glad some things never changed.

His gaze settled on a small table with a blue enamelled coffee-pot. 'Mind?' He nudged his head towards the pot. 'Been in the saddle a mite long and breathin' that dust you New Mex folks call air.'

Marshal Glover's grin widened. 'Air tastes a damn sight better'n that coffee of mine, but help yourself.'

Jim went to the table and poured coffee black as a killer's heart into a tin cup. Taking a sip, he winced. 'Christamighty, Uncle Frank, last time I tasted somethin' this bitter I had bit clean through a roach that crawled into my beans!'

'You always were a belly-acher, son!' Frank Glover lowered his body into the chair behind his desk, a weariness crossing his face as he relaxed. Better than sixty years showed on his lined face. His hair tended more towards steely grey than the brown it had once been and his forehead nearly met the horseshoe-shaped bald spot at the back. Jim somehow didn't recollect his uncle looking that old but it had been a few years since he'd last ridden through the territory.

'A belly-ache is just what I'll have drinkin' this horse manure.' He grabbed a hard-backed chair and dragged it in front of the desk. Straddling it, forearms braced on the back after he set his cup on the desk, he peered at his uncle. 'No disrespect, but you look tired, Uncle Frank. Law business too much for those old bones?'

'Well, this is a cattle town, son. We got our share of hardcases and rustlin's. Sometimes it's hard to keep up.'

Studying his uncle, Jim saw a certain weariness in the older man's eyes. 'You ain't tellin' me the half of it. Reckon you been havin' your hands full with something.' His tone grew more serious.

'Well, I cain't sheep dip you, son. Been havin' a time with one of the ranchers 'round here. Man name of Rutherford Stark thinks he can swaller up everything and every one. He's been givin' a rancher and his daughter a saddle-full and I reckon he ain't done with them by a long shot. He's run me ragged with false claims against them, as well as against a few other folks he's been hasslin'. Most folks just gave in and sold their land to him cheap, else he plumb scared them into leavin' it.'

Jim sighed, running a finger over his upper lip. 'And this rancher and his daughter ain't pullin' stakes?'

Glover shook his grey-tufted head. 'I gotta admit I admire them for stickin' to their guns, but I'm afraid sooner or later there'll be some kind of trouble that ain't so easily fixed.'

'Reckon this man Stark might make some charge stick? Hurt them?' Jim knew the type and it sent a prickle of irritation down his spine. Powerful men took powerful notions and sometimes their means to an end was somewhat south of the law, especially in these parts.

'Wouldn't put it past him. He's damn sure pointed an accusing finger in their direction enough times. But I'm afeared of worse. Stark, he's . . . ' The marshal's gaze went distant.

'He's what?' The younger man's eyes took on a look of curiosity and his sense of compassion for the underdogs strengthened. He had always felt that empathy with the oppressed; that was what had set him on his trail in life in the first place. For Jim Sutter was a manhunter, a free agent who hired himself out in the name of justice.

'Well, he's a coward, I figure. A coward without a conscience and maybe that's the worst kind. I reckon he never gets his hands dirty, least that anyone can see.'

'But you wouldn't put it past him to hire someone to do his dirty work . . . someone like me?' A bitterness in his voice caused his uncle to flinch.

'Hell, no, son! That ain't what I am sayin' at all. You got your britches on right side out. What you do, you do in the name of somethin' higher, a sense of justice and virtue.'

Jim gave a humourless laugh. 'Sometimes I got to wonder if it's anything so noble.'

'I know you far too well to know it's anything but, son. You got a burnin' inside you to do what's right. Don't you keep second guessin' yourself.'

Jim smiled a lop-sided smile. 'What makes you think I do?'

The marshal uttered a belly laugh and Jim felt a prickle of irritation. 'Learned to read men more years ago than I can count, son. Recollect I'm the one who taught you to use your gun, too, when you came in all starry-eyed with that dime novel 'bout some famous gunslinger you admired to high horse hell. You took a notion to be just like them heroes in your books. Bet you got one in your pocket right now.'

Jim relaxed, realizing his uncle was right. He had started out that way and was still that starry-eyed boy with a burning sense of right and wrong in his soul. Sometimes. Other times . . . well, he had questions that needed answering.

'Reckon you know me too well, Uncle Frank.' He pulled a dime novel from his pocket and tossed it on the desk.

The marshal glanced at it and laughed. 'From the looks of its condition it's probably been read a few hundred times.'

'Manhunters spend lots of nights on the trail and my horse ain't a hell of a conversationalist.'

Marshal Glover chuckled, then his face went serious. 'You killed a man yet?'

Jim's belly sank and he stood, feeling the need to move about. The memory of bringing down that one fella who refused to come peaceable still haunted him. He wondered if maybe that was when things had started to change for him, caused him to question his direction, look ahead at the fork in the trail and be confused as to which one rode towards the sunset.

'One . . . ' His voice came out a sombre whisper.

'Felt like hell, didn't it?' The marshal's face grew sympathetic and Jim's grew remorseful.

'Felt like someone poured hot lead down my gizzard.'

'Man deserve killin'?'

'Reckon, as much as any man does. Just gotta wonder now if it's my job to decide that.'

'Who would you leave the decision to, son?'

'Lord, maybe. Dunno.'

The marshal let out another belly

laugh and Jim felt the pique return. 'Lord only decides after you send them to 'im, son. Someone on earth's gotta lay down the sentence. Way I see it, it might as well be someone with a sense of justice like yourself than a man like Rutherford Stark.'

'Ain't that a marshal's job?'

Another laugh, and this time Jim felt some of the irritation dissolve. 'I'm just a cow town marshal, son. Small bull in a big stampede. If I don't go along with what is I get trampled. You . . . you don't have to go along, least not as rigidly. Me . . . well, I'm old and I do what's right, but I ain't got a hell of a lot to back it up nowadays.'

A thin smile played on Jim's lips. 'Don't sell yourself short, you old bastard. You got what it takes and always have. You'd stand up to that stampede if faced with it.'

Marshal Glover frowned. 'Reckon I wonder if I would . . . ' He studied the younger man a moment. 'Hell, you never answered my question — what brings you this way? You hired out to someone in this area?'

'No, no case. Reckon I'm just passin' through. Was thinkin' of lookin' into maybe buyin' me a spread or staking claim to a mine.'

'You serious, son?'

Jim shrugged. 'Maybe not. Maybe I'm just startin' to feel the seams in my saddle.'

His uncle studied him and a knowing smile came into his eyes. 'Hell you are, son. You're more serious than you think. Where'd that starry-eyed boy go?' He picked up the pulp novel then slapped it back down on the desktop. 'The boy who always had one of these under his nose when he was s'posed to be doin' chores?'

Jim let out a saddled laugh. 'Left him behind somewhere on the trail, Uncle Frank. Reckon every man does that after a time.'

'Reckon. But not you. Leastwise I never thought you would.' His uncle peered intensely at him, a questioning light in his eyes. 'Maybe it's somethin' else?'

'What are you drivin' at?' Jim shifted feet, belly cinching, and looked out through the dusty window.

'Well, you're getting on near to thirty-five, now. Young compared to me, but for a manhunter . . . '

He glanced back at the marshal. 'Hell there's plenty old manhunters!' he said with false indignation. 'Ain't felt a bit of a slow down.'

'Ain't you? Ain't talkin' speed, son. You made it all them years without killin' a man, then that day came and now you figure your hands are slicked with blood. Maybe it's slowed somethin' inside you you ain't wanted to face.'

'You puttin' me out to pasture already, Uncle Frank?'

'I'm puttin' you out to life, son. If you've lost that desire, you best get out of the business. Manhuntin' ain't no game for a doubtful man.'

'That all you were getting' at?'

The marshal's face went thoughtful. 'Not entirely. Maybe you need to settle down with some filly and raise yourself a passel of young'ns 'fore you're past the age.'

It was Jim's turn to belly laugh. 'You ain't serious, are you?'

'Damn straight I am. Trail is a lonely place. When's the last time you had a woman?'

'Been a spell. Never was much one for whores or passin' through relationships.'

'Lots of things to see and do in this world, son — while you're young. When you get older, well, those lots of things ain't so important any more and you wind up lookin' down a mighty lonely trail.'

Or two . . .

Jim sighed. 'Reckon I *have* looked down it a few times, more so lately.'

'Betcha have. I been a lawdog all my life. Don't know nothin' else and never had me the time for a woman. Wish I had now. When I retire there ain't nothin' for me. Ain't nothin' to go home to but a passel of memories and a worn tin star. Hell of a thing to look forward to.'

Jim turned back towards the window, something inside him clutching, aching, wondering. He struggled to force it down with little success.

Movement outside broke his reverie and his gaze centred on a rider coming down the shadowy street. The rider guided a roan in a deliberate, sombre gait that reminded Jim of a funeral march. A patch of cidery light cast by a hanging lantern fell over the rider's features and a twinge of surprise took him. A woman. The sorrowful expression darkening her face more than the fact of her gender was what gave him pause. That expression told Jim she was a woman in a heap of hurt and trouble.

A half dozen yards later it was plain where she was headed.

Jim looked towards the marshal. 'You got company. And it don't appear to be a social call.'

'Lordamighty, what now?' The marshal hadn't come half out of his chair before the door opened.

Jim's gaze went in that direction. He studied the young woman who came in. Despite the dark half-circles nesting beneath her eyes and redness within, she was a vision. Possibly four years his junior, she carried herself with a posture of self-sufficiency and maturity that surpassed her years and belied the strain evident on her features. Pulled-back blonde hair accentuated the solid beauty of her face. Dressed in a simple gingham blouse and divided skirt with shot sewn into the hem, her figure, full of bosom with gently flaring hips, was easy on the eyes.

'Ma'am . . . ' The marshal tipped an index finger to his brow. Jim, folding his arms, remained silent, saw her glance at him, the glance lingering, probing, and what — damning?

Her gaze shifted back to the marshal. 'My father . . . ' She faltered and Jim took a step towards her, to offer a hand.

She quickly regained composure and waved him off. 'No, mister . . . ' Coldness laced a voice that under other circumstances he reckoned would have sounded as lovely as a summer dawn.

'What happened to Cyrus, Ruby?' The marshal took a step around the desk, but stopped when she gave him a halting look.

'He's . . . dead, marshal. Killed.'

Shock deepened the lines on the marshal's face. 'Killed? Cyrus? Christamighty . . . ' Glover's voice dropped to a whisper, and Jim got the distinct impression his uncle had just faced the ghost he knew had promised to haunt him. 'How?'

Shuddering, the woman took a moment to compose herself. 'It was murder, plain and simple, marshal. I want the man responsible brought to justice and hanged.'

'Ma'am, just take a deep breath and tell me what happened,' the marshal prodded.

She glanced questioningly at Jim,

back to the marshal. 'Who's he?'

'That's my nephew, ma'am, Jim Sutter.' He looked at Jim and nudged his head at the woman. 'This here is Ruby Pendelton. I was tellin' you 'bout her and her pa and their ranch earlier.'

Things suddenly coalesced in Jim's mind and not with any comfort. What his uncle feared *had* come to pass: someone had raised the ante and struck at the rancher in a devastating fashion.

'Man showed up and called my father out, marshal. Just came ridin' in and called him out.' A tear leaked from her eye and she quickly brushed it away, as if letting them witness her display of emotion were some kind of sin.

Incredulity slapped the marshal's lined features. 'Called him out? Your pa's near to seventy years! Who the hell calls out a seventy-year-old man?'

'A fella Rutherford Stark sent to kill him. Man named Vinton Stroud.'

The name echoed like a shot in the room. Jim's heart stuttered and the marshal's mouth plain fell open.

'Hell and tarnation . . . Who'd you say, ma'am?' the marshal asked, as if he hadn't believed his ears.

'Fella's name was Stroud. Vinton Stroud.'

'Ain't no mistake about that, miss?' Jim felt a shiver skitter down his spine.

She glared at him with a look of annoyed indulgence. 'Ain't no mistake, Mr Sutter. It is not a name I am likely to ever forget.'

'Ma'am, you know who Vinton Stroud is?' The marshal still seemed not to believe what he had heard.

'He's a killer, marshal. That is all I need to know.'

The marshal shook his head in disbelief and sat heavily on a corner of his desk. 'Why would a man like Stroud call your pa out? That don't seem his style. A man like that — '

Fury flashed in her eyes, strengthening her resolve. 'A man like that does what he is paid to do, Marshal. You know that as well as I do. Rutherford

Stark hired a mankiller to murder my father because we wouldn't sell our land to him or scare off easily.'

'Now, ma'am, we got no proof it's Stark — '

'The hell we don't! What more proof you need? That sonofabitch has been tryin' to get our land since God created it and you know it. Was just a matter of time till he tried somethin' worse.'

'But hirin' a shootist to do murder ... ' The marshal seemed to deflate, shoulders sagging, and Jim knew he believed the girl's suspicions, despite Stroud's reputation and the lack of clear evidence.

'He hired him, marshal, and you know it. Ain't no ifs or ands about it. You go arrest Stark and this Stroud, then find the nearest cottonwood and stretch their necks.'

A pained look touched Glover's face and Jim knew what was coming. The law was bound by certain constraints and procedures, even out West where conduct often fell far short of what the

East considered civilized. Frank Glover had always held a deep abiding respect of his profession and duty; no matter how much he sympathized with Ruby Pendelton or accredited her story he would uphold that integrity now.

'I'm powerful sorry, ma'am, but I can't just arrest him on what you've told me. Ain't that I don't believe you, it's just that I pledged to uphold the law even when it ain't quite what I'd like it to be. I can question Stroud when I find him, but it's goin' to come down to his word against yours.'

She glared. 'I don't rightly see how. My father's the one with lead in his chest.'

Jim had been through this enough times with his uncle to ask the next question. 'Did your pa try to draw his gun, Miss Pendelton?'

She shifted feet, refusing to look at him, and her voice grew colder. 'Stroud gave him no choice, Mr Sutter. He would have killed him anyway, likely me as well.'

The marshal shook his head, features going more grim. His tone softened with apology, but it failed to take the sting out of his words. 'If Cyrus attempted a draw, Miss Ruby, Stroud will claim it was a fair fight and what you're tellin' me will back him up. As for Stark, well, I'm willin' to bet Stroud won't implicate him. Stark wouldn't have risked hirin' him otherwise.'

'Then you're tellin' me you will do nothing?'

'No, that ain't what I'm sayin' at all. But I am sayin' it's more complicated than just arresting him. Stark's a powerful man in these parts. It'll take a lot of evidence to make somethin' stick.'

Her face dropped and Jim felt sorry for her. He also felt his sense of righteous duty surge up and struggle to take over. It was the one thing he had always felt was real, touchable within him: the justice. The need to help someone who needed it.

'Maybe I can help you, miss. I ain't

so bound by legalities.'

She glared at him and her gaze sent a chill down his spine. 'I don't need *your* help, Mr Sutter. I've seen quite enough of the kind of aid your type offers for one day.' Her gaze swept back to the marshal, challenging. 'If you'll do nothing I will, marshal. That's a promise. He gave me a week to be off my land and turn it over to Mr Stark. That means I best get myself prepared.'

The marshal frowned. 'Stroud actually told you Stark sent him?'

'He did.'

'He ain't likely to admit that if you question him,' Jim put in. 'Still be her word against his.'

'I don't need your opinion, Mr Sutter,' Ruby said in a dismissing tone without even glancing towards him.

'But he threatened you, Miss Pendelton — '

'He has gone beyond threatening, Mr Sutter. He has murdered my father.'

She turned, glancing at Frank Glover as she gripped the door handle. 'I reckon I'd best wake the funeral man, marshal. I may expect you to pay your respects at the buryin'?' Her words came with a tremor of anguish.

The marshal gave a short nod. 'I will talk to Stroud, ma'am, and get to the bottom of this. I'll see justice is done.'

She let out a strangled laugh. 'Will you, marshal? Will you treat Rutherford Stark and Vinton Stroud the way you did my father and me when we were accused?'

'Don't catch your meanin', Miss Ruby.' He caught it all right and Jim saw it plainly on his face. She wanted to know if the wheels of justice turned the same way for a lowly rancher and his daughter as they did for a powerful cattleman like Stark.

'You catch it, marshal.' She banged the door closed behind her. For long moments neither the marshal nor Jim said a word.

Jim broke the silence. 'You believe her, I can tell.'

'Hell, yes, I believe her, but that don't mean my hands ain't tied.'

'You can do more than just question Stroud or Stark.'

'I got limits, son. Neither of them are like to be confessin' any time soon and strongarm tactics don't serve to do more than irritate fellas like that. And like she said, her pa made an effort to defend himself.'

Jim let off a scoffing laugh. 'A seventy-year-old man against the likes of Stroud?'

The marshal's gaze dropped and Jim saw shame and self-disgust in his uncle's eyes. 'Stroud's a highly respected bounty man.' His voice was low, words drained of conviction.

'Then what the hell's he doin' with a man like this Stark?'

The marshal's gaze lifted. 'Reckon I don't know. But Stroud . . . he's hell on a saddle.'

'But you still figure Stark hired him to take Pendelton and his daughter off their land . . . ' It was not a question and the marshal reluctantly nodded his affirmative.

'Stroud don't come cheap. Stark has the means. Fella has a reputation that's almost mythical.'

Jim went to the rack and grabbed his hat, placing it on his head. 'Usually find myths are just that.'

'Where you goin', son? You got that Galahad look to you again.'

'To talk to Ruby Pendelton. Maybe I can do somethin' for her. Like you said, I ain't reined in by the letter of the law.'

Or fear . . .

'Careful, son. I got no hankerin' to be goin' to your funeral, too. Stroud's reputation is more than just what's written in your books. He's the real thing. Got himself a gun they call the Devil's Peacemaker. Thing's delivered more redemption than a hell and damnation preacher. He's never lost.'

'Ain't no such thing as never, Uncle Frank.' Jim said it with more flippancy than it deserved. ''Sides, I got me a few surprises in my saddlebags.'

'You'll need 'em.' The marshal turned to the desk and picked up the novel, looked at Jim. 'You'll be wantin' to take this.'

Jim frowned, as if he were somehow leaving a piece of his past behind. 'You keep it. Maybe there's less truth in those things than I thought . . . '

As Jim left the marshal tossed the book on the desk and sighed a weary sigh. Lantern light fell over the title and a chill shuddered through him. '*The Life and Times of Vinton Stroud*,' he mumbled, the words dying in the silence that crowded the room.

3

The Silver Spur saloon was as packed with patrons as a railcar stuffed with longhorns. A heavy pall of Durham smoke clouded the room. The air stank of sweat and dung, old vomit and sour booze, and Vinton Stroud savoured every sweet breath as he gazed around at the cowhands playing chuck-a-luck and poker, dominoes and Monte.

Shouts punctured the haze, as men threw down winning hands; their profanity sizzled the bar-room when they lost. Tinhorns crowded green-felt tables and soiled doves in plunging bodices or peek-aboo blouses clung to winners' arms, their creamy bosoms ripe for plucking and offered for four bits a pleasure. Their counterfeit laughs annoyed him, though these days there rightly wasn't too goddamn much that didn't. As his gaze swept over the doves,

he searched for the one called Lenore
— her name was something else, Stark
had told him, but hell if he could keep
it straight in his mind — whom he
would be dealing with shortly.

Gaze moving on, he saw a stairway
leading to an upper level of rooms and
cubicles where doves did their deeds.
He wondered if she were up there.

Clumps of old sawdust crunching
beneath his boots, he threaded his way
towards the long bar running east to
west. 'Whiskey.' He slapped a silver
dollar on the bar top. 'Make sure it ain't
watered or worse. I ain't forgivin' of
bad redeye.' The look he gave the 'keep
made the man replace the first bottle he
had pulled off the shelf and reach for
another with deeper-coloured liquor.
Stroud grinned beneath his soup-
strainer mustache and the barkeep
visibly shivered. Stroud enjoyed seeing
that. Fear was a potent elixir, after all,
nearly as sweet and erotically satisfying
as killing. An easy laugh escaped his
lips. How he loved to kill. How he

relished the gunmetal scent of ripe blood and the vacant look in his victims' eyes as death extinguished life. How he revelled in the elation that burst through his veins like dynamite exploding. Little or big, man, woman or child, it rightly made no nevermind to him.

It was his essence, he rightly figured. His true nature and duty, and even Stark would realize that someday soon. Vinton Stroud seldom worked long for men like Stark. They were all basically cowards, afeared to get blood on their hands. They hired others to do the killing for them. But sooner or later those men stepped over his personal boundaries of justice and, well, like he said, killing tasted sweet.

Lately, though, he was pained to admit he'd felt an increasing flatness to his killings. A diluted sense of satisfaction he rightly didn't cotton to. It took more and more death to satiate the craving.

He reckoned that was because the

killings had simply come too easy. Rarely did any fella offer him a challenge that would make the fever rise higher, burn more intensely. Most men couldn't compete with his lightning draw, his iron nerve and deadly accuracy. But that, he was forced to admit, took some of the fun out of it, the intoxication. Hell, the outcome was damn near predestined.

He downed a slug of whiskey and made his way to a table. Lowering himself into a chair, he tossed his hat onto the table-top. Gaze sweeping the bar-room, he again searched for the dove Stark claimed tried to cheat him out of her pleasures and took his roll and a few belongings to boot. *Lenore.* Forever lost Lenore . . .

A spike of pain stabbed his temple and he tensed, waiting, dreading what might come, but it passed with only a few beads of sweat springing out on his forehead.

He probed in a pocket and brought out a battered leather-bound book. He dragged his fingertips over the cover, feeling its roughness. He traced the gilt letters, *The Complete Poems of Edgar Allan Poe*, savouring their smoothness. He opened the book, gaze flowing over the sacred words.

' 'Deep into that darkness peering — ' ' The words came out a whisper.

'Game, gent?'

A prickle of irritation took him as a voice invaded his reverie. He looked up with a goodly measure of vexation in his eyes to see a vested tinhorn holding a worn set of cards peering down at him. Unperturbed, the man riffled the cards in his spidery hands, a gold ring holding a blue stone on his right index finger flashing with captured lantern light. Stroud's gaze settled on the gambler's gaunt face and a sense of loathing twisted in his belly. The blackleg's nose was a map of veins and his teeth were jagged. His chin came to a sharp point and the fellow reminded Stroud of a buzzard. Under most circumstances that would have made him no nevermind.

But one of his eyes . . .

A devil's eye, milky and leaking, unseeing. It never moved, though the fellow's other orb did. It disgusted Stroud, made him want to pluck it out, fry it up with mountain oysters and devour it.

'Reckon I ain't much in the mood, fella.'

The man scrutinized him, the milky eye remaining fixed, staring straight at him, boring into his soul.

'Well, hell's bells, gent, course you are! You got the look of a fella who could give me a good game and not bat an eye at puttin' up some real stakes. You ain't one to shrink from a challenge are ya, gent?'

That damnable eye . . .

Stroud couldn't pull his gaze from the man's mucousy orb. Revulsion grew stronger within him. 'Sit down.' The words were stony, a command not a request, and a flicker of unease flashed across the tinhorn's buzzard face. He hesitated, licking his lips.

'I said, sit down . . . ' Stroud didn't have to repeat it again.

The tinhorn sat and shuffled the cards. 'Game's draw poker, jacks or better to open, check and raise permitted. Five dollar ante, bettin' limit of ten, no more than three raises allowed. Any objections?'

That eye . . .

'None.' Stroud tucked the Poe book back into his pocket and pulled out a roll of greenbacks, then set a stack of silver dollars on the table and portioned aside five dollars' worth. 'Original rules, no straights or flushes.'

The blackleg dealt, fingers now evidencing a quake. Not once did Stroud remove his gaze from the godawful eye. The orb transfixed him, burned its hideous gaze deep into his soul.

Pluck it out . . .

Time seemed to vanish as the game went on, greenbacks and clinking silver filling the pile in the middle of the table. The expression on the mankiller's face remained stoney, never changing.

'Card?' The tinhorn tapped the deck.

Tap-tap-tapping . . .

'What?' Stroud had barely heard him. Instead a muffled cacophony rose from somewhere deep in his skull, like the throbbing of a heartbeat.

'Said, you want another card?' The tinhorn's bottom lip danced.

Stroud took another slug of whiskey, swiping a forearm across his lips.

Tap-tap-tapping . . .

'No.' His tone came cold and steady, final. The throbbing beat in his skull grew louder, louder, louder.

The gambler's tongue wandered over his lips. 'Call 'em.'

The throbbing grew sharper, aching, and his eyelids fluttered. Pain stabbed deep into his temple.

Tap-tap-tapping . . .

Stroud stared at the eye, as he lowered his hand and fanned the cards on the table. That oyster eye peered inside him, dissected his cataracted soul and reflected it back.

He saw ghosts in there, spectres of the men he had butchered, the women, the lives burned down under his lead. He saw them all, beckoning to him, calling out his name and damning him for the evil thing he had become. Sweat broke on his forehead, trickling down his face.

Pluck it out . . .

'Two pairs, eights and treys . . . ' Stroud's voice came low, challenging. The gambler peered at his hand then at the pile of silver and greenbacks lying in the middle of the table. A flash of doubt crossed his buzzard features.

'Well, gent,' the tinhorn's voice held far less confidence than it had when he asked for the game. A hesitation stuttered the descent of his cards to the table. 'I see you're a hell of a player, but I must say there ain't many a fella can beat old Jared Briggs.' The man fanned his cards down, his good eye roving, the bad one fixed straight on Stroud. 'Four kings, ace high.'

Stroud's black eyes narrowed. 'A miracle hand, Mr Briggs . . . ' Stroud said it with the tone a hangman uses on a condemned hardcase.

The gambler tensed, mustering false bravado. 'I reckon I am a man of miracles, gent.' He began to rake the pot towards him.

'You might need another one now . . . '

Tap-tap-tapping . . .

The tinhorn stopped and focused on the mankiller, fear a rabbit in his eyes.

'Hell.' Stroud snapped out a hand and grabbed the tinhorn's wrist. Something beneath the man's sleeve felt solid, more solid than bone and muscle. The blackleg yelped and Stroud glared at him.

Ungently rapping . . .

'You cheated, fella.' The accusation came cold and convicting.

'The hell I did!' The man spat the words indignantly, half-rising. Stroud's grip clamped about the other's wrist like a steel band. The man winced, face pinching with pain. 'Jared Briggs don't need to cheat to win, gent. No, sir, he don't.'

'He did this time.' Stroud rose, still gripping the tinhorn's wrist and pulled him from his seat. His gaze never left that mucous orb.

That eye . . .

'Hey, what the hell — ?' the tinhorn bleated, genuine panic lacing his tone.

With his free hand Stroud grabbed the man's sleeve and tore it free, revealing a spring-loaded holdout designed to snap a card into the wearer's palm when needed.

The gambler began to shake. Stroud saw fear dancing in the sharp's good eye. Its fiery nectar sizzled in his veins. This was a bonus, for one old man and a whore would never be enough to quell the bloodlust. Stroud would relish closing that eye for good. He swore he could hear the fella's bones rattling as he shook with fear.

Tap-tap-tapping . . .

Realization dawned in the man's good eye. The blackleg knew he had made a mistake that would cost him his life if he didn't try something fast.

Stroud anticipated he would.

'Surely a gent of such breedin' and unlimited understandin' can see his way to forgiveness and mercy . . . ' The tinhorn's free hand slid towards his vest and Stroud let it, a knowing smile on his lips. The pounding clamour in his skull began to recede.

That eye . . .

' 'All that we see or seem is but a dream within a dream . . . ' ' he whispered, gaze locked to the man's deformed orb.

'W-what?' the tinhorn asked, more a gasp than a word. Sweat streamed down his buzzard face. His hand halted at a vest pocket, spidery fingers prying deep and easing a derringer —

The raucus hullabaloo came to a dead halt, as a shot thundered in the saloon. Bawdy laughter stifled and

58

heads snapped around, startled expressions slapping the faces of cowhands sober enough to realize what had occurred. The barkeep's mouth dropped open and his gaze roved. Silence fell hushed and heavy.

Stroud released the tinhorn, whose fingers were still tightly clenched about the handle of a Remington .41 'Double Derringer'. The man crumpled to the floor, a cloud of sawdust billowing up and settling over him. A gaping hole in his belly pumped blood and Stroud eased the Peacemaker back in to its holster, a thin smile on his lips. Bending down, he removed the ring from the man's index finger, straightened.

The gambler's good eye fluttered closed, but Stroud felt a revulsive chill as the other mucous orb continued to stare straight at him . . .

★   ★   ★

'Miss Pendelton!' Jim shouted, as the young woman stepped from the funeral man's place and walked towards her horse. She paused, appearing momentarily alarmed, until realizing who he was. A flutter of nerves butterflied in his belly. Ruby Pendelton didn't care for him a lick and that made him vaguely reluctant to approach her, but the need to offer his assistance outweighed that. What his uncle had said was true, at least partially, that in this case the law had its hands tied. A manhunter could offer more.

As he walked towards her, the chill night air tingling his face, she faced him with a look of grim challenge. 'What do you want, Mr Sutter? The marshal knows Rutherford Stark and Vinton Stroud are responsible for murdering my father. What he wishes to do about it is now up to him. I have my own concerns to think about.'

His gaze met her and he saw the pain in her eyes, the haunting loss. He also saw defiance and strength, maybe a certain recklessness he read in himself sometimes.

He frowned. 'What are those concerns, Miss Pendelton? If they involve going after a man like Stroud then — '

'Then what, Mr Sutter? Then I should just act all ladylike and refrain from any fool-headed notions I have about goin' after him? Let him take what's rightfully mine?'

'He's a master shootist, Miss Pendleton. He's outgunned some right tough *hombres* and put a lot of bad men in the boneyard.'

She glared at him, eyes hardening. 'I see reverence in your eyes, Mr Sutter. You respect this man, this murderer, don't you? You hold him up as some sort of hero.'

The venom in her voice brought a surge of guilt to his heart. He had indeed held Stroud up that way, but it was the Stroud in those novels he had read countless times, Stroud the living legend. The reality appeared to clash with the myth.

'To be honest, Miss, I've read a lot

about him and it seems to dispute what you're sayin'.'

Anger flashed across her hazel eyes and she locked her arms together. 'Then why did you bother comin' after me, Mr Sutter? To tell me what a hero Vinton Stroud is? To tell me how he's made the West a better place for us simple folk? Or to tell me he's the most righteous sonofabitch to ever come down the trail and call me a liar?'

He shifted feet and looked at the boardwalk, unsure how to respond for one of the few times in his life. Something about this woman played hell with his confidence.

His gaze came back up. 'I ain't callin' you a liar, Miss Pendelton. I'm statin' simple fact. Everything I read about this Stroud led me to believe he was something special, a legend, and maybe that was wrong. I'm offerin' to find out, maybe give you some peace of mind.'

She let out a scoffing laugh laced with both incredulity and anger. Turning on a high-topped shoe toe, she strode to her horse. Gripping the horn, she yanked herself into the saddle. She cast him an anguished look that made his innards clutch.

She took a shuddery breath and a tear wandered from her eye. 'Peace of mind, Mr Sutter? My father's dead. I'm alone and have one week to live unless I give up everything that's mine to a man who's no better than the one he sent to kill my father.'

'I'm sorry, Miss. I was just tryin' to help — '

'You go to hell, Mr Sutter. You go straight to hell and take Vinton Stroud and all the rest of your type with you.'

Her words stung like whiskey on a snakebite. He suddenly wondered why he even gave a damn what this woman thought of him and why it cut so deep. 'What type might that be, Miss Pendelton?' He regretted the question the moment her face tightened into an accusative mask.

'Why, a killer, of course, Mr Sutter. A

no-good murdering sonofabitch like the fella you so graciously offered to help me with.'

She reined around and rode off, using the same funeral gait she had ridden in with.

A killer.

She knew, somehow. She knew he tracked men and brought them to death, by rope or by lead. She labelled him no better than Stroud. Manhunter or murderer; it was all the same to her.

Did his profession show on him that much? Did he wear it like a goddamn badge of some sort, a badge of retribution and death like some damned dark angel?

He got no time to think about it. A shot rang out, jerking him from his thoughts. He started, spinning, hand going to the handle of his Peacemaker. The sound had come from the direction of the saloon. A hushed silence filled the street.

A door burst open. His uncle stepped onto the boardwalk and glanced towards him, a grim question on his face.

Jim ducked his chin towards the saloon and both headed in that direction.

'Reckon we ain't had enough excitement for one night.' Jim's voice held nearly no tone.

Glover frowned. 'Be willin' to debate that, son.'

They shoved through the batwings, stopping just inside. Jim's eyes narrowed as he scanned the bar-room.

'I ain't yer goddamn Lenore!' a dark-haired dove with Mexican features shouted. Jim's gaze swung towards her. A man in a black duster gripped her wrist; she struggled but was held fast.

Jim followed the marshal deeper into the room, gaze settling on a body lying in a pool of blood on the floor. Coldness trickled through his being and his attention went back to the man holding the girl.

'Let her go!' Glover's voice was sharp, perturbed.

The shootist turned his sights towards them. 'Marshal . . . ' The man's coat swung aside as he turned. Jim saw the Peacemaker with the carved relief of a ram's head, awe taking him for just an instant. He knew he was now face to face with the man he had read about so often in those dime novels, the legend who carried the Devil's Peacemaker. He was forced to admit the fella had a presence about him, a commanding force that seemed to reach out and intimidate. He inspired fear, though Jim felt none. Fear was an emotion he left behind the day his parents died and he would not give in to it now.

'Let her go, I said.' Marshal Glover's hand rested on the handle of his own Peacemaker.

Dark eyes narrowing, unreadable, Vinton Stroud looked at the girl, who gazed back with a mixture of fright and fury. She yanked her wrist free, the impression of Stroud's fingers in her flesh remaining in blistering red.

She backed away, rubbing her wrist

and flashing Stroud a look of utter contempt. Reaching the stairs, she spun and hurried up, disappearing somewhere on the upper level.

'You responsible for this, Stroud?' The marshal nudged his head towards the dead tinhorn.

A thin smile poisoned the mankiller's lips. 'You know who I am?'

'Don't everyone?' Jim couldn't hide the mixture of hero worship and suspicion that laced his voice.

Stroud scrutinized him, dark eyes probing, attempting to intimidate, and Jim felt the urge to take a step backward. He held his ground. While unnerving, something about the man's black gaze rang false, something . . .

Insane?

Whatever it was vanished as Stroud looked back to the marshal. 'Who's the sidekick, marshal?' The mankiller's hand drifted to a coat pocket, bringing out a gold ring with a blue stone. He slid the ring onto his finger, but it didn't seem to fit quite right, in Jim's estimation. He took the sinking notion it had belonged to the dead man.

'I asked you if you killed this man, Mr Stroud. Would appreciate an answer.' Did Jim hear a slight catch in his uncle's voice? He reckoned he did. His uncle was intimidated by Stroud, though making an effort to hide the fact.

Stroud nodded. 'I killed him. He cheated and tried to draw on me. Derringer's still in his hand. If you look on his wrist he's wearin' a holdout as well. Reckon those facts put me within my rights for punchin' his ticket.'

Jim and the marshal's gazes shifted to the dead man, noting the small weapon clutched in his fingers and the card cheating device strapped to his wrist.

'You sure 'bout those details?' The marshal eyed Stroud, this time unwavering. He took the law seriously, Jim knew, and no measure of fear would alter that.

'Sure as I'll ever be, marshal. Reckon any number of folk in here can attest to that fact. Way I see it, self-defence pure and lily.'

'Any of you say different?' the marshal asked the cowhands and doves in the room. Each voiced agreement with Stroud, even the barkeep.

'Reckon that seals it, marshal.' Stroud's voice came smug. He grabbed his hat from the table and placed it on his head.

The marshal held up a halting hand. 'Just hold your ponies, Stroud. I got me a few more questions I aim to ask you. You ain't leavin' till they're answered.'

Stroud looked vaguely annoyed, but didn't move.

The marshal held Stroud's gaze. 'You out at the Pendelton place earlier tonight?'

Stroud's face tightened a notch. 'Reckon I was, marshal. Had me some personal business to 'tend to there.'

'Cyrus Pendelton was a fine man, Stroud. You had no right gunnin' him down.'

'Was he?' An eyebrow lifted. 'I figure he was a horse thief and no-good land swindler. That gave me every right to punch his ticket.'

'He was old. You knew he'd never be able to out-draw the likes of you.'

Stroud gave the marshal a look that said something Jim wasn't sure of. A threat?

'Man's a horse thief and land stealer. He went for his gun. Makes no nevermind to me whether he was ten or a hundred, slow or fast. I hit what I aim for.'

'I know better'n that, Stroud. That man never stole anything in his life, neither did his daughter. That land belonged to him fair and square, despite any claim to the contrary.'

'Beg to differ, Marshal. He took land that didn't belong to him and refused to give it up. He drew on me and probably that pretty filly daughter of his'n will back that story up.'

The marshal seemed to deflate. The

look on his features said he knew Stroud had him and there was damn little he could do about it. 'Stark hired you to go after him?'

Stroud chuckled; there was nothing humorous in the sound. 'Stark's my cousin. I'm visitin' a spell and he told me 'bout his problem. I just went to pay a friendly visit and the fella braced me. All there is to it, Marshal. Ain't a man who can say different, in my estimation.'

Not a living one, anyway, Jim amended.

'Best you ride on back to wherever you came from and let Mr Stark fight his own battles, Stroud. Really ain't no need of you here in Holliday.' The marshal's gaze locked with Stroud's.

Stroud looked at the upstairs level and smiled. 'I got me some business to conduct in your town, Marshal, an' like I said, I'm visitin' my cousin. I'll leave when I'm ready to leave and there ain't much you can do 'bout it, 'less you got some charges you can make stick. Way I see it you don't.'

Stroud stepped between them, brushing Jim's shoulder as he did, and walked through the batwings.

After the gunslinger left, Glover eyed Jim and the younger man shrugged. 'Wasn't much you could do at this point, Uncle Frank.' He tried to sound sympathetic but the marshal's eyes held disgust.

'Sometimes I wonder why I'm still marshal, son. Sometimes I just know a man's guilty and I can't do a damn thing about it when I should.'

'You keep the law. That's the best you can do.'

'Do I keep it, or run from it?'

Jim glanced at the batwings, wondering about the man who had just left. Legend or killer? Saviour or butcher? 'Stroud's got somethin' in his eyes. It ain't quite right, but he covers it up well. I've seen enough guilty men to know the difference and that man's . . . ' What? He couldn't quite put a finger on it.

'That man's a killin' lookin' to happen. Reckon we ain't seen the last of him or the death he brings.'

Jim sighed. 'Got a notion you're right.'

4

'You're up a mite early,' said Marshal Glover as Jim Sutter came through the office door. Outside false dawn painted the October skies in shades of gunmetal grey and a layer of frost coated the windows. Lantern light threw jittering ghosts across shadowy office walls and deepened the lines on Glover's face. Or maybe that was more a mix of worry and fear on his uncle's features rather than any trick of the light, Jim amended. Whatever the case, it didn't suit the lawdog well. His uncle wasn't the type to let frettin' get the better of him, as it plainly was now.

'Hell, that sorry place this town calls a hotel has beds as hard as a whore's heart.' He tried a smile that didn't work.

The marshal made a wavering off gesture. 'Could always tell when you were lyin' to me, son. You damn well know that.'

Jim's smile became genuine. 'Reckon you always could. You ain't puttin' nothin' over on me, either. You look like a week on the trail. Bet you slept as much as I did last night.'

The marshal sighed, nodding. 'Can't deny it. That thing with Stroud's been eatin' at my innards. Hell, if it were just some tinhorn gone boots up I wouldn't give it much nevermind. That type comes through a cowtown like Holliday all the time. When Stroud says the fella was cheatin' I'm inclined to believe him.'

'You reckon Stroud was tellin' the truth and the gambler drew first?'

The marshal nodded. 'Reckon. Reckon it don't matter a lick either way 'cause no one in the saloon was about to say different.'

Jim ran a finger across his upper lip. 'What about that dove he was holdin' onto when we walked in?'

'Camilla Espita. Been at the saloon a

spell but doubt she'll stay. She's got a shark look in her eyes and I reckon if we took a closer look we'd find she's supplementin' her trade with other pastimes, stealin', swindlin' cowhands. She's heavy on the laudanum it looks to me and that don't come cheap.'

'Why you think Stroud was holdin' her? He didn't have the attitude of a fella lookin' to get his bells rung.'

Glover shrugged. 'Who knows? Maybe she just threatened to tell a different story where Jared was concerned and wanted to blackmail him. If she did, she picked the wrong fella to try that on.'

'Reckon she's in any danger from him?'

The marshal's brow furrowed. 'Them type is always in danger. If she crossed Stroud some way I wouldn't be surprised if we ain't puttin' her in the back of a wagon. Other hand, it's likely nothin'.'

'She ain't what you're worried about, that it?' Jim's gaze drifted out the

76

window into the street. The rising of the sun was splashing yellow-orange light over the buildings. Early October gold coated the dust and sparkled from water troughs. Frost on the office window melted and ran in watery glimmering streaks.

'Hell, no. My mind's on Stark and Ruby Pendelton and what Stroud might do to her.'

'Spent half the night thinkin' on that myself.' Jim turned back to his uncle. 'She needs help, but she refused me outright. She's got some bee in her bonnet 'bout me bein' a no-good killer like Stroud and I ain't rightly sure I can change her mind.'

The marshal nodded, face more grim. 'I saw it in the way she looked at you last night. Just as well, though. If you're got yourself a hankerin' to get off the trail Stroud certainly ain't the last saddle you want to mount. Stark, neither, for that matter. You'd be better to just get your mind off both of 'em *and* that girl.'

'Reckon my notions on Miss Pendelton are strictly business.'

'That so? You sure those stars ain't back in your eyes, son?'

'Phshaw! Just my sense of justice, Uncle Frank. You know how I get. I want to help her even if she don't want to accept it.'

'You just try an' convince me that's the only thing you got in mind. I been around too long not to see the makin's of a fine romance.'

Jim scoffed, but felt more uncomfortable than he thought he should have. 'Christamighty, Uncle Frank, my life's complicated enough as it is.'

'Well, it got more complicated by a damn sight when you came back to this town. Wish you were tellin' the truth about that woman, though. I don't want to be seein' you in a pine box, way her father ended up.'

'How you figure?'

'You get too close to her you get too close to Stark and Stroud. That ain't conducive to a peaceful retirement.'

'Hell, the West in general ain't particularly good for that. Reckon my mind's made up already. She needs help and I aim to provide it, whether she thinks I'm a cold-blooded killer or not.'

The marshal sighed. 'Don't s'pose I could talk you out of it?'

Jim raised an eyebrow. 'Could I talk *you* out of it?'

'Don't catch your meanin'.' It was Marshal Glover's turn to look uncomfortable. He squirmed in his chair and averted his gaze.

'You don't really want to let what happened with Stroud and Stark yesterday go. I saw it last night. You feel powerful bad for that girl and you feel the injustice of what happened to her father. You're scared, though, Uncle Frank. Maybe more scared than I ever saw you before, but you got that same sense of justice I got in me. You want to help her, too. You want to offer her more.'

The marshal sighed a weary sigh,

resignation on his face. 'Awright, you've pegged it, if that makes you feel better. I do care, but I'm damn close to pasture time and I'd like to spend my days on some nice river bank whittlin' little animals out of chunks of pine.'

Jim uttered a scoffing laugh. 'Hell you would!'

Some of the tension eased from the marshal's face. 'You might be right at that.'

Jim's face went thoughtful and he took a sip from his cup. 'Why don't you tell me more 'bout this Stark fella.'

'There's a lot to tell. He's a powerful man in these parts. Stark came by his wealth without the hard work most cattlemen go through. He inherited a bundle and used it to buy folks in positions of power from what I hear, set himself up right nice on the blood and sweat of others. Recently he started buying up all the land he could get ahold of in the area. Squashed a number of smaller outfits or plain scared folks off them.'

'Ambitious to a fault?'

'Puttin' it mildly. He made them legitimate offers, though. Many a folk jumped at the chance; the ones who didn't sold out after a bit of persuadin'.'

'What kind of persuadin'?'

'Things happened to their ranches, cattle got rustled, a few outbuildings caught fire, veiled threats, that sort of thing.'

'What about this business with Pendelton?'

'Cyrus was a hell of a man but stubborn as a mule with a notion not to move. Stark made him the same offer he made the other ranchers but Cyrus refused to sell. Cyrus gained title fair and honest before Stark was a glint in New Mex's eye and set himself up a fine little spread.'

'Cattle?'

'No, Cy never took an interest in cattle. He had himself a blacksmithin' business in his barn and Ruby raises some fine horses and makes dresses for the ladies here in town. Cyrus wanted a peaceful life to raise his daughter after his wife, Jesse, passed on and that's just what he was doin' till Stark came along.'

'I take it Stark didn't cotton to Cyrus's refusin' to sell?'

'Not a lick. Cyrus's land is right smack bang in the middle of Stark's expansion plans. Stark's got himself a notion his britches are bigger than Chisum's and he ain't about to let no mule-headed rancher ruin his plans. He wants what he wants and damned if a body should be in the way.'

'So he just removes them . . . '

'Removes them and never gives it a second thought. Ruthless bastard.'

'But one who coats his dung with gild and shines just as pretty as can be.'

'That's the size of it.' Marshal Glover paused, as if collecting his thoughts. 'Anyhow, without Cy's land to connect two tracts Stark owns to either side he won't have an easy access to the rail comin' through here next spring. He knows it, too.'

'So Stark started pressuring Cyrus?'

'Yep, a shed burned down one night, some corrals got messed up another. But Cyrus still wouldn't budge. I was worried Stark might try burnin' him out completely but maybe that pointed a bit too much his way for comfort.'

Jim raised a questioning eyebrow. 'Hirin' Stroud didn't? That's not exactly subtle.'

'Well, maybe not, but Stroud's a fall guy whether he knows it or not. Stark could always claim he was actin' independently and it would be his word against the mankiller's.'

'Stroud don't impress me as anyone's fall guy. Stark might have jumped on an owlhead horse there.'

'Stark ain't the smartest *hombre* to come down the trail, but he's good at manipulatin' folks and situations to his end. Power and money seem to fall in his lap. Some fellas are just like that.'

'Reckon William Bonney thought that way 'fore Garrett put a bullet in him. Comes around sooner or later.'

Glover raised an eyebrow. 'You got a notion to make it sooner?'

'Reckon I got an itch to help his end along.'

'Reckon he'll have the same notion for you once he gets wind you're doggin' him. Reckon you'll never see him comin', neither, 'cause he'll send Stroud to do his dirty work.'

Concern hung in his uncle's voice and Jim conceded the older man had a point. A man like Stark would stay in the shadows while Vinton Stroud carried out a sentence of execution. Did he have a chance against the mankiller? He'd never seen him in action; many of his feats might be nothing more than a writer's imagination. But somehow he doubted it. After meeting Stroud last night he reckoned the man likely deserved every lick of his reputation.

Jim frowned. 'So Cyrus Pendelton wouldn't sell and Stark had him killed. Quite a step up from scare tactics.'

'Sure as hell is. He tried some other things, sendin' men in here claimin'

Cyrus had stolen this or that, that Ruby's horses belonged to his spread and she had altered the brands or hired some Indian artist to do it. Nothin' ever stuck, of course. Was mostly just harassment stuff, makin' a nuisance out of himself to Cyrus. Even claimed the land belonged to him and Cyrus had stolen that. That's still a burr in my britches.'

'Why? Cyrus held title, you said.'

''Cept then Cyrus kept his title in a bank box and you might say Stark has the bank man by the balls. Boils down to the fact that Cy's title went missin'. Little doubt Stark was behind it.'

'Must be copies, original seller's, whoever handled the transaction?'

The marshal nodded. 'Original owner went East after sellin' Cyrus the land. Ain't been able to find hide nor hair of him and believe me I looked. Injuns might have got 'im. Somethin' sure did, because he never arrived at where he said he was goin'.'

'What about whoever handled the transaction?'

'Well, that's a bit more problematic. See the deal was handled by a lawyer named Dubias Phinney. When I went to see him he claimed he had no idea where the title copy was and didn't recollect handlin' the deal.'

'So Stark got to him, bought him off?'

'Yep. Reckon Stark planned to have Phinney turn some fancy legal cartwheels and put a claim to the land by callin' in a few favours of some muck-a-mucks Stark has in his pocket.'

'You think Stark's got the titles?'

'I'd lay bet on it. Cyrus thought so, too.'

'Then why kill Cyrus? If Stark was plannin' somethin' like that, why not just wait?'

The marshal leaned back. 'I wondered that myself. Came up with a couple of reasons. Whatever Stark planned it would take time and if it didn't happen by next spring things might get more complicated. Was a chance Cyrus might have gotten it straightened out by then, too. Stark likely couldn't afford that risk, so maybe he wanted the old man out of the way to ensure the land became his. He probably figures Ruby would be easier to scare into sellin', 'specially with her father gone.' He paused, eyes thoughtful.

Jim studied his uncle, seeing something else in the older man's eyes. 'You reckon he had another reason, though?'

Marshal Glover nodded. 'Like I said, Stark's a vicious coward. He don't like bein' said no to. I think when Cyrus refused to sell it set somethin' off inside him and he wanted to get even.'

Jim's brow knotted and disgust twisted in his belly. 'So he hired a professional gunslinger to kill a seventy-year-old man?'

'Stroud said he was Stark's cousin. Maybe he called in a favour. Whatever the reason, Stroud took on the job, I'd bet my life that was Stark's motivation.

He's a cold-hearted bastard.'

Jim considered his uncle's theory regarding Stark and felt his disgust grow. Here was a man who had all he ever needed, land, money, power, yet he wanted more, and he didn't care if he had to murder an old man and his daughter to get it.

'You look somewhere on the trail, son.' His uncle's voice cut through his woolgathering. 'You also look like your wheel's startin' to come loose.'

Jim sighed, a depressive mood taking him. 'Sometimes I wonder about the West, Uncle Frank, the men who make it. Plenty of decent folk sacrifice everythin' tryin' to build themselves a life but they just end up in a box. Then there are men like this Stark fella who don't care a lick about others. They just take whatever the hell they want and go on about their merry way. Why not just let them have that whole damn thing? Sometimes it just don't seem worth fightin' it; it just don't seem to matter.'

'Don't sound much like the boy I

taught law to. You always took a notion to uphold those folks' rights, such as they are.'

'What difference have I made? There'll always be men like Stark, with their dung-coated aspirations and dirty schemes.'

'Without men like you, and me, maybe, that'll never change.'

'We're a drop in the trough, Uncle Frank. A good man like Cyrus Pendelton gets murdered because of land. A fine woman like Ruby Pendelton might end up that way as well.'

'Hell, son, you're puttin' me in a spot. On the one hand I want you to just ride on out of here and set yourself up nice with a little spread and live your life till it's done. I know you been givin' it plenty of thought. That's why you came here.'

'Yet on the other?'

'Yet on the other, I know I damn well can't handle Stroud and Stark alone. Ruby Pendelton can't, either. Stark will take her land, make no mistake about it. If she gets out with her life she can consider herself a shade luckier than her father. Stark will go on about his business knowin' he can just take whatever the hell he wants when he wants it and never have to pay for it with his sweat and blood, way honest men do. The West needs men like you, son, though I damn well don't want you goin' after Stark and Stroud and endin' up dead. Ruby Pendelton needs a man like you, too.'

'She'd likely disagree.'

'She don't know the difference 'tween you and Stroud right yet. She lumps all manhunters into Stroud's pile of dung. She'll come around, though.'

'So you askin' for my help?' A mischievous light danced in Jim's eyes and he felt the dark mood lift.

'Hell, no! I'm tellin' you to ride on out of here and take Miss Ruby with you, if you can get her to go. Make yourself a peaceful life that don't involve men like Stark and Stroud and swallowin' lead pills.'

'You got a lie in your voice, Uncle Frank. You know if I ride out Stark wins. That sticks in your craw as much as mine.'

The marshal sighed. 'I don't think you can beat Stroud, son. I won't honey-coat it. He's the devil.'

'He's a man, Uncle Frank. Maybe more skilled than most, but that don't change the fact that he bleeds like any other.'

'Ain't so sure he's a man. I saw somethin' in him last night when he looked at that girl and that dead gambler. Took me a spell to place it, but I finally did. The man plain enjoys killin'.'

Jim thought it over. Maybe that's what he had seen in Stroud, that elusive glimpse of the man's soul that branded him a cold-blooded killer. 'I'm inclined to agree. I practically worshipped his tales when I was younger. Saw him as a counter agent to men of Stark's ilk. But the reality of it . . . well, it don't swallow easy, let me tell you.'

'Leave him be, son. Please.'

'You're still speakin' out of two sides of your mouth, Uncle Frank. You're afeared of him, but I think you're itchin' to go after him if he gives you a solid reason.'

'I hope you ain't right, but I'm afraid that might be it.'

'You also got a notion if anyone can stop him it's me.'

Glover sighed, nodded reluctantly. 'I taught you all I know and you took it beyond that. In my younger days, who knows? I was damn fast, but you were faster from the get go. Faster than Stroud? I don't know. But you got somethin' that man either ain't got or has no longer. You got a sense of what's right and that sometimes makes up for all else. This case, though, it might not be enough. All told, you're best to ride on out with your life, and Ruby's.'

'Phshaw! You really think I got a chance in cowboy hell of convincin' her to leave that land?'

His uncle looked at him long and hard. 'No . . . reckon I don't.'

'Then I reckon my direction's clear, Uncle Frank.' Jim stood and went to the door. Opening it, he paused, looking out at the warming day.

'Son . . . '

He turned and peered at the strained face of the man who had guided him, taught him, knowing that man was begging him to leave before it was too late, yet at the same time asking him to see justice was administered where it was needed.

'Mind's made up, Uncle Frank. Reckon you know that well as I do. Doubt you'd try to seriously convince me otherwise even if it weren't.'

Marshal Glover let out a defeated sigh. 'It ain't no fun bein' a confused old man, but I reckon you're right.'

Jim smiled an easy smile. 'Hell, it ain't no fun bein' a confused young one.'

'Watch your back, son. You might

have picked up some tricks out there on the trail, but Stroud likely picked up more.'

Jim tried to sound reassuring. 'First thing you ever taught me, Uncle Frank. Never forgot it.'

The day had warmed, the chill of the October night dissolving under a brassy sun climbing the sapphire sky. Days like this could almost make a body forget about men like Stark and Stroud and think only of a woman like Ruby Pendelton and settling down to a new life.

He felt a longing to just ride out and let life wander over him, fill him with peace and contentment, dispel the confusion and show him which trail to ride. But the feeling was fleeting. He could never turn his back on Ruby Pendelton and let Stark take what was hers; he had taken far too much already.

His boots clomped hollowly on the boardwalk as he walked towards the telegraph office a few blocks down.

Holliday was laid out in roughly a T shape and during the day looked like any other cowtown, peaceful, if bustling. 'Hands from local ranches rode in for supplies while cattlemen's wives arrived to peruse the latest shipment of dresses or trinkets from back East, for flour and coffee or any other staples needed. Only at night did the town burst alive, offering its dubious vices to weary 'hands eager to oblige.

Beyond the town, in a horseshoe pattern, lay the flanking cattle spreads, most owned by Stark, he reckoned. Far in the distance, on a diagonal ten o'clock course, lay scattered mining settlements gone bust, the abandoned silver strike town ironically named Eldorado being the largest, which wasn't saying a hell of a lot. As many men had perished under the false gilded dreams of gold, silver and copper strikes that had never panned out, as had been trampled under the hooves of Stark's cattle empire.

The way Ruby Pendelton might be

trampled. Unless he could do something about it. He reckoned a few
queries to a Pinkerton friend might be
the best place to start.

His thoughts settled on the young
woman, as he strolled towards the
telegraph office. She stood no chance
against the likes of Stroud and Stark.
He judged her to be a solid woman of
the West, self sufficient and strong as
she was beautiful, but she would be
removed like any other opposition that
stood in Stark's way. Could he
convince her of that? To simply turn
tail and pull stakes? He doubted it. She
wanted her father's killer brought to
justice and would fight for what was
hers. The odds against didn't matter;
she was willing to buck them. While
Jim admired her stand, at the same
time he worried it might lead her to do
something foolish. He could temper
that, if she let him, use his skills to
even those odds. It would take careful
planning, and he would need to
become the red cape of a bullfighter to

the bull, divert Stark and Stroud's attention away from the spitfire of a woman and onto himself.

Unfortunately, she had made her mind up on another point that made any strategy in that direction problematic: she despised what he was, what he stood for, and it galled him, burrowed under his skin in a way he had never experienced. Hell, he couldn't blame her for thinking that way after what happened, and maybe he had no right forcing his help on her, but neither could he leave her to fight Stark and Stroud alone.

Christamighty, what was happening to him? Things used to be so clear cut. Yesterday he had ridden in with meandering thoughts of settling down. Since arriving in Holliday the confusion had grown immeasurably. He was starting to question himself more and more, even questioning his sense of duty, pondering what good he was doing. It wasn't like him, not by a damn sight. He hired out his skills and tracked down hardcases, turned them over to the law for hangin' or imprisonment. All nicely packaged and never a second thought as to the wherefores or the whys of the West that produced them. Why were things changing so fast now? Was it that man he had killed, the ensuing nights he had lain awake simmering with guilt, regret? Was it coming face to face with one of those legends gone bad? Or was it more than that? Maybe he could blame all of that, but a nagging suspicion told him Ruby Pendelton had the biggest part in it.

Reaching the telegraph office, he came from his thoughts. As he entered, a man behind the counter looked up from beneath his visor.

'He'p ya, stranger?'

Jim nodded, taking a slip of paper and writing out a message. 'Would be much obliged.'

Vinton Stroud. He wanted to know more about the man, the things one didn't find in the pages of pulp novels.

He had some questions about Stark as well.

Finishing the message, he tossed a greenback onto the counter, thanked the man and went out, wondering just how wide the gap between the legend and reality of Vinton Stroud really was.

★　★　★

The telegraph office door rattled open and the man behind the counter looked up. No doubt he thought the young fella who'd been in here a few minutes earlier had forgotten something, or wanted to send another message. When the man's eyes focused on Vinton Stroud, he knew different. Vinton waited for the effect to take full measure, letting his Devil's Peacemaker show as he brushed back the flap of his duster.

It had been a piece of luck, he figured, comin' in this morning before the sun even came up. He had spent much of the night at Stark's, annoyed he'd been deprived of a third kill last night. He had let the marshal get the better of him, but, hell, he couldn't just waltz in and bury the local law, least not right off.

But that other fella . . .

Riding in an hour before false dawn, he had waited in the dark shadows of Holliday, finally spotting the young man he had met last night go to the lawdog's office this morning. He had planned on waiting the entire day if necessary, but Old Nick had provided him with a break. Something he had seen in the fella's eyes last night told him this man might prove to be a bigger obstacle to Stark's plans than the Pendeltons would ever be. He had seen the type before and disposed of as many. Men who had a sense of duty, of righteousness. Those men always wound up buried. The price of integrity in the West was death, wasn't it? Hell, the price of everything was death. That young fella would be no different, but he might provide something sorely lacking in Vinton Stroud's killings lately: a challenge.

'That fella who just left here . . . ' Vinton's gaze pinned the telegraph man. The operator tried to shrink into his chair as Vinton took slow steps towards the counter. 'What'd he want?'

The man gathered a bit of courage. 'He, he wanted to send a telegraph. That's what anyone who comes in here does, send one or pick one up.'

'Best watch your tone, friend. I got kind of an intolerant mood on today.'

The man swallowed and a muscle in his cheek twitched.

'What do you want?' he asked, voice breaking.

'I want a copy of what he sent.'

'That there is privileged information.' The operator's tone held little conviction.

Vinton grinned and suddenly his Peacemaker was jammed against the man's forehead. 'You might say this makes me privileged.'

101

★   ★   ★

After stopping at the hotel to retrieve his saddlebags, which he had slung over a shoulder, Jim made his way towards the livery.

The sun had climbed higher and the day had turned quite warm for October. He wondered if his query would turn up anything on Stroud or Stark. He had a feeling a man like Stark covered his tracks pretty well, but Stroud was another story. The shootist, he bet, didn't care who found out about him, because he'd simply remove them when they did.

Reaching the livery, Jim halted. He would have to wait a while for the results of his inquiries and in the meantime he saw two possible moves. He could confront Stark, question him, flash that red cape, or he could work on convincing Ruby Pendelton she needed his help. He bet that would prove about as easy as trying to persuade Stroud to pack up and move on. Another forked trail, he reckoned. He smiled. He had decided on the more difficult of the two: Ruby Pendelton.

He entered the livery, the scent of hay and dung and leather combining into a pleasant musky odour. Going to a stall, he stroked his horse's snout. The bay nickered contentedly.

'Hell, Ruthie, what's a gal like Ruby Pendelton doin' stuck in my mind anyway? She plain hates the ground I walk on and gettin' involved in her hassles means gettin' involved with Stroud and that's likely the wrong fork to take.' The horse lifted its head as if nodding agreement and Jim frowned.

'You been alone too long, son,' he muttered, hearing his uncle's tone in his mind. Maybe he had. He had been with a few women, mostly saloon girls in weak moments and he wasn't particularly proud of the fact, but something about Ruby Pendelton set his innards to fluttering.

Was the need for someone in his life, someone who meant something, stronger than the drive to dispense justice? He had blamed his questions on that killing before; he couldn't deny that had given him a turn. Until that point, he had always been able to take his men alive, letting the law dole out the punishment. He had never avowed to the same creed most manhunters did: the only way to end injustice was to shoot it between the eyes.

He had never thought much about killing when his uncle taught him to shoot a Peacemaker. He supposed it had always lurked in the back of his mind somewhere, the knowledge that some day someone would force him into an irrevocable situation. He'd even practised a special move he liked to call the pitch-and-draw, in case that time came. The move, wherein he would pitch suddenly right while pulling his gun, was designed to increase his chances of walking away from a gunfight alive, though it remained unproved since that fella had not given him the chance to use it.

He worked hard on other skills, learned safe cracking from a fella in El Paso, roping techniques from another in Matadero, all designed to provide him with an edge, reduce the odds of having to take a life. For the most part it had worked, and he had become adept at manoeuvring men into positions of surrender.

He had always known somewhere inside he would kill if forced to. And he had. It had burned like holy hell in his soul.

What would Ruby Pendelton think of a man who killed, even if it were in the name of justice?

The answer seemed obvious on the face of it. While he couldn't blame her, he figured she at least owed him the chance to explain, to make her see the difference between him and Stroud.

A sudden thudding pain exploded in the back of his skull and he knew instantly he had just made one of the biggest mistakes of his life: he'd forgotten to watch his back. Stars

cascaded across his vision and blackness threatened to flood in and eclipse
his senses. Legs deserting him, he went
down.

He hit hard, face slamming into the
hay-strewn ground. The shock jarred
him back to his senses. His head
whirled as he struggled to get up.
Pushing himself to his hands and knees,
he lifted his head to see who had hit
him.

A boot heel crashed into his mouth.
Shards of pain sliced across his lips and
rattled through his teeth. He coughed a
spray of blood. The force of the kick
propelled him over and backwards.
Landing flat on his back, he stared at
the beamed ceiling through blurry
vision.

A laugh. A laugh like none he had
ever heard. Harsh and low, pregnant
with menace and mockery.

'Want to go for your gun, boy? Got a
notion to test your mettle?'

A voice, jeering, challenging, coming
from just to his left. He pushed himself

to his elbows and tried to focus on the dark figure leaning against the stall. The man had his duster pulled back, hand resting on the handle of an ornately carved Peacemaker.

The Devil's Peacemaker.

'Stroud . . . ' His voice came out shaky. Blood trickled down his chin and its gunmetal taste soured his mouth. Disgust welling, he knew he had let himself get too distracted by thoughts of Ruby Pendelton when he should have been watching his back, way his uncle taught him. He should have realized the mankiller might take an interest in him after last night, might stake him out to discover if he posed any threat. It was pure textbook and he was damn lucky Stroud hadn't taken the notion to just blow his brains out.

Stroud's dark eyes narrowed. 'You got a hankerin' to know about me, boy? I'm here to tell ya. I killed a hundred like you, maybe, fellas who had more gumption than they had skill. Fellas who figured they knew what true justice was.' Stroud paused, spat. 'You got that stink about you. The stink of right. West don't work that way, boy, and the slower you learn that the quicker you get buried.' Stroud stopped, drilling him with those black eyes, the eyes of a soulless killer.

Jim suddenly knew what Stroud was all about. The mankiller had let him see into his black soul. He was no legend, no hero of pulp novels. He was a brutal beast of prey, an inhuman monster who relished killing. The man tracked and destroyed, likely with little reason other than to fulfil his own addiction to blood.

'You're loco, Stroud.' Jim's words came out almost a whisper.

Stroud shrugged. 'Might say that about any man who makes manhuntin' his business.'

'You murdered Cyrus Pendelton for Stark. Likely you killed a lot of other innocent folk.'

'Some folks just need killin'.' Stroud peered closer at Jim, a strange glitter in his black eyes. 'Men like you make me sick — Sutter, is it? You go around the West preachin' 'bout how things should be different and damn few times you got the skill or the balls to back it up. You got your goddamn sugary notions about fair play and justice and how life should work out right. You got it all figured out, don'tcha? You can just ride in on your goddamn white horse and make things better for decent folk. I'm here to tell ya, boy, it ain't that way an' it never will be.'

'What about men like you Stroud? Goin' around murderin' folks. That make anything better in your estimation?'

Stroud laughed. 'Hell, boy, it makes no nevermind to me if things get better. I just feed the fever.' Stroud took in a deep breath, a deranged expression lighting his face. 'Can ya smell it, boy? There's fresh blood out there just waitin' to be spilled.'

'You're a cold-blooded bastard.' Jim

spat the words, and Stroud uttered a derisive laugh.

'You ain't the least bit afraid of me, are ya? Hell, I like that. I just might let you live a bit longer because of it. I need me a challenge, Mr Sutter. You might say my work has lost its lustre. Killin' has become too easy. But you best have sand and skill, Mr Sutter, if you plan on kickin' my wood-pile.'

Stroud pushed away from the stall and began to walk from the livery stable. He paused, keeping his back to Jim. 'Reckon I know your type too well, Mr Sutter. I know you don't back-shoot and I also know you don't let threats shake your direction. But if you got any notion of helpin' out that Pendelton woman or buckin' me you might think it over real careful like.'

With a laugh Stroud walked through the doorway. The day seemed to absorb him. Jim watched him go, almost wishing he was the back-shooting type.

5

The encounter with Vinton Stroud had left Jim's body aching in more places than he cared to think about. His skull throbbed with a vengeance and his mouth pained like he'd been stamped on by a mule.

Stroud had gotten the jump on him all too easily. It goaded him. He should never have turned his back on someone like that, even figuratively. Of course Stroud would consider him a possible threat, and take measures to determine such. Any manhunter worth his salt would. Jim let out a curse, disgusted with himself for making a foolish mistake, one that had damn near gotten him killed.

Stroud. The man was plain loco. Jim was convinced of it now. The shootist enjoyed killing, revelled in bloodshed and that was all there was to it.

The killer had warned him to stay away from Ruby or face the consequences. Hell, a sane man would have turned tale and run right then, but Jim had not even considered it. He had shakily saddled his horse and climbed aboard, going through with his original intent of trying to convince Ruby she needed his help.

You're a damn fool! He had told himself that more than once after sending the bay towards the Pendelton ranch. With the sparkling air of the warm autumn day and aroma of falling leaves scenting the breeze it would have been so easy to just turn around and find a more peaceable — and healthy — way to earn a living.

He reined up, taking in a deep breath. Around him the countryside was deceptively tranquil. To look at it he would have never suspected so much death and sorrow lurked close by, stalked Ruby Pendelton, and now him. Trees rose to either side of the trail, which skirted a nearby stream. He heard the murmuring of its gentle flow and the shushing of the breeze through leaves touched with red and yellow and orange. Under other circumstances it might have filled him with a sort of spring fever.

After his encounter with Stroud, however . . .

He sat straight in the saddle and ran a finger over his swollen lips.

Stroud.

The Devil's Peacemaker.

The devil's mankiller.

A hundred yards on, foliage and trees fanned out, thinned into graze land and rolling hills and he surveyed the roughly circular pattern of a small shiplap ranch house and stable, scattered corrals, a couple of sheds and outhouse. It wasn't much to speak of, compared to the larger cattle spreads, but likely Cyrus and Ruby had built most of it with their own hands over a period of years and it was something he reckoned he'd be right proud to settle on.

Hell, what are you thinking? he

chastized himself, slipping into the wanderlust pattern again. Hadn't being pistol-whipped by Stroud taught him dwelling on might-bes or gilded dreams was damn dangerous?

He gigged his horse into an easy pace, ambling along the stream to his right. A sound took his attention; he looked up to see a startled dove flutter from the brush near the stream. Something had disturbed the bird and his gaze traced its path, halting on the figure of a woman who was staring out at the bubbling water. As if sensing his presence, she turned and looked straight at him. In the midday sunlight she was a vision, despite the lines of grief etched into her face. Sadness dulled her reddened eyes, the half-circles beneath deeper than on the previous night. Dried tears had left tracks on her cheeks. He wondered how long she had been out here.

Guiding his bay towards her, he drew up, wishing he knew what to say to her that would bring comfort, ease the pain. A woman like that belonged smiling, the joy of life dancing in her eyes.

'Ma'am . . . ' He tipped an index finger to his Stetson.

Bitterness flashed in her eyes. 'You come to kill me, Mr Sutter?'

The question stung. He shifted uneasily in the saddle. 'Beg your pardon, Miss Pendelton, but that's a hell of a thing to ask.'

She scrutinized him, as if knowing her words had pricked him and wondered why. 'Maybe it is, Mr Sutter, but I reckon with what I've been through it's not so far out of reason.'

He nodded. 'Reckon you got every right to be angry.'

'I got more right than that. I got a right to hate all your kind.'

'Why you dislike me so much, ma'am?' He reckoned the best approach with a woman like Ruby Pendelton was direct and honest. It was the only chance he had at gaining her respect.

She folded her arms and her hazel eyes narrowed with bitterness. 'Dislike you? Is that what you would call it?'

'Well, you seem to have me all tied up in a nice little package with the likes of Stroud 'fore you got a right to.' He stepped from the saddle and stood holding the reins.

Her eyes flamed with anger and he knew he hadn't helped his case much. 'My father was murdered by the likes of your type, men who kill for the sheer thrill of it. You're a manhunter, Mr Sutter. I knew it the moment I laid eyes on you. You got it in the way you carry yourself, that all-powerful attitude that hangs on you like skunk piss.'

Jim felt a prickle of irritation. 'That's a mite harsh, ain't it? You got me judged when you don't even know what I stand for.'

'Do I? Then tell me, Mr Sutter — what is it you stand for? What justifies killin' men for money?'

He hesitated, unsure of himself. 'I don't kill men for money, Miss

Pendelton,' was the best he could think of saying.

'Then what do you call it? Enjoyment? Sport? Isn't that what you get paid for, tracking down a fella and puttin' him out of someone else's misery?' She eyed him with cold challenge, daring him to say different than what she believed.

'Hell, ma'am, when you put it that way — '

'What other way would you have me put it, Mr Sutter? Tell me! I want to know. I want to know what makes men like you think they can play God Almighty and choose life or death for another.'

He shuffled, gaze shifting from the intensity of her eyes to the stream, watching it meander along like his life seemed to be meandering. He struggled to collect his thoughts, find something that would change the way she perceived him, but he saw no way to honey-coat it. His gaze locked with hers. 'I don't kill men for money, Miss

Pendelton. I bring them in and let the courts and law decide their punishment. I do what I think is right.'

She studied him, as if searching for any sign of a lie and for an instant he thought he saw a slight wavering of her conviction. 'How many men have you killed, Mr Sutter?'

She gazed at him as if everything hinged on this one answer, and if he lied she would know it. 'One,' he admitted in a low voice.

'And that makes you different from Stroud? Sheer numbers? Is one man's life taken worth less than twenty? Thirty?' The words came harsh and accusing, but did he detect a hint of a difference in tone, a softening? A need for explanation? Maybe. From her expression she plainly believed he was telling the truth.

'No, it don't make me better. That man drew on me and forced me into something I didn't want. I gave him a clear chance to come peaceably and he refused to take it.'

'So you killed him?'

'I had no choice. He would have killed me.'

'And you figure that justifies it?' Her tone went harsher again and he wondered just what she wanted from him, what she was looking to hear, and why.

'Nothing justifies killin', if that's what you're askin'. I rather it would have never happened, but it did and I can't change that. I've regretted it ever since. It gives me nightmares and makes me ask questions of myself even you might appreciate.'

She uttered a derisive laugh. 'What kind of questions would those be, Mr Sutter? Somehow I doubt I'd appreciate anything about you.'

Her tone said different and he found himself strangely eager to tell her. Despite her hostility towards him, he wanted her to listen, to understand what he was, who he was, and why he was.

'Makes me question what I'm doin',

why I am doin' it and if I want to keep on doin' it. Makes me wish I had a choice more often than I do.'

Her eyes softened a notch. She was weighing his words, perhaps granting him the benefit of her doubt. 'You have a choice, Mr Sutter. We all do. My father chose to go against someone like . . . ' She stopped, voice brittle, cracking with emotion.

'Like me . . . ' he completed.

She turned away, to look out over the stream. A quiver shook her body and he wanted to go to her, take her into his arms and tell her that everything would be all right, that he would make Stroud pay for taking her father and make everything in her world fresh and new again.

But he felt frozen, locked in indecision. He knew she wouldn't accept comfort from him, not right now, perhaps not ever. And it was a promise he couldn't make in good conscience. The outcome was too unsure. Stroud might kill him, and even if he brought the renegade bounty man down nothing in her world would ever be fresh and new again. She could only live with what had happened, strike an uneasy truce.

'Just sayin' you got a choice, Mr Sutter. We all do and maybe lots of the time that choice is the wrong one.'

'Reckon you're right. Reckon I wonder that more, now.'

She turned, a tear slipping down her cheek. 'Do you?'

He bowed his head, looked back to her. 'God's honest truth.'

A moment of awkward silence passed and he could hear the gurgling of the stream and the sounds of birds twittering in trees. He wondered if he had made headway with her, gotten through in some small way, and prayed he had. He wanted to go to her, feel her lips on his, her body in his arms. But mostly he wanted her approval, or at least her tolerance for what he was, what he stood for.

'You're hurt . . . ' Her words came

low and trickled away, lost within the sounds of the day; he swore he heard compassion in them.

'You might say Stroud and I had a minor difference of opinion.'

'He attacked you?' Her eyes narrowed.

'I decided to check on some of his past activities, along with Stark's, and wired a Pinkerton friend about them. He saw me do it, I reckon, got my name from the telegraph man and came after me. Hit me in the back of the head and put a boot in my mouth. He ain't the play fair type.'

'Are any of you manhunters?' The venom was back in her tone and he suddenly wondered whether he'd made any headway at all.

'Can't speak for others, Miss Pendelton, but I'd never shoot a man in the back.'

She studied him, searching for any sign of deception. 'No, I don't believe you would.' She bent and tore a swatch from her skirt, then went to the stream and dipped the cloth in the water. Folding the cloth as she came towards him, she dabbed the dried blood from his swollen lips. It stung like all hell, but he didn't pull back.

She pulled the cloth away and their gazes locked. She gazed at him with an openness he would not have expected, letting him glimpse the hurt she felt, the suffering, the loss, and revealing a little girl softness and vulnerability. He suddenly longed to press his lips to hers, experience the fire of her kiss. He wondered if she would accept it . . .

Hell, that was foolishness! If she wouldn't accept his help she damn well wouldn't want him kissing her. Still he didn't pull back and she didn't turn away or avert her gaze. Each seemed frozen in the moment.

The urge to draw her into his embrace, kiss her grew overwhelming and he pulled back before he couldn't stop himself. Legs shaking like an infatuated schoolboy's, he stepped into the saddle. Gathering the reins, he peered down at her. Her eyes still held that openness mixed with grief.

'I plan on goin' after Stark and Stroud, Miss Pendelton. I plan on helpin' you keep your land whether you want that help or not.'

He expected her to flat out refuse, but she remained silent. He wondered if maybe something *had* changed between them. He reined around and gigged his horse into an easy ground-eating gait. If he were going to help he reckoned he needed to do more than just enquire about Stroud and Stark. He was going to have to kick a few wood-piles, as Stroud had put it. And that would start now . . .

★ ★ ★

Ruby watched Jim Sutter ride away, an odd sense of regret and loss washing over her. She hadn't expected the warm feelings growing within her. She had wanted to hate him, take all her bitterness for Stroud and Stark and focus it in his direction. But she couldn't, because she knew everything he told her had been the truth. She would have caught any lie. She thought perhaps she had misjudged him, curiously found herself hoping she had.

She felt some doubt still, however. It was hard to reconcile the caring noble man she had just spoken to with the fact that he had killed a man. Tracking men was his business, and he believed in what he did. But she was no fool, either. She knew manhunters as a whole were an unsavoury lot, many little more than reformed outlaws or glorified killers like Stroud. But Sutter . . . maybe he *was* different.

His face rose in her mind, his deep-blue eyes. He possessed a gentle and somehow shy manner. Yet beneath that was a strength of character she had seldom seen in men, especially in Holliday. She saw compassion and nobility within him. That certainly did not live within the black eyes of Vinton Stroud. So perhaps she had been in error and he wasn't like Stroud, and perhaps a man like Sutter had his place in this grim West after all.

Something else surprised her: she had wanted to kiss him. Despite her bitterness and pain and all he stood for in her eyes, she had wanted to press her lips to his, to fall into his arms if only for a moment and let all the cascading grief and searing pain escape in a rush of tears and sobs and unadulterated weakness. Only for a moment, but it had stunned her, frozen her.

She glanced back towards the house that seemed somehow alien to her now, gloomy and vaguely threatening. She'd been unable to face going back there last night and today, returning to its barren rooms and haunting emptiness. So she had stayed by the stream, despite the chill biting through to her bones and freezing her tears, despite the hunger that gnawed at her belly. She had slept not a wink and spent the time letting the creatures of the night hear her sobs. She hadn't given a damn if

Rutherford Stark or Vinton Stroud simply rode up and shot her brains out.

Damn you, Ruby Pendelton! she admonished herself. Was that the way Cyrus Pendelton had raised his daughter? Was that the way he would have wanted her to go on? Not by a damn sight, she reckoned. He had reared her to be self-sufficient and tough as old leather, after his image. She was the son he had never had and at times he damn well forgot she was a girl, then a woman. She knew that wasn't entirely his fault. It had been hard on him after mom died and he had done the best he could do.

She wrapped her arms about herself and gave in to a shudder. If Cyrus were guilty of anything it was neglecting one thing, that she was still a product of both of them, Cyrus and her mother, Jesse, and that made her softer than he, less iron-willed when it came to going on alone in this world. Although she had been but a child when her mother passed on, she remembered the scents of perfume and the feel of lace and a little doll fashioned out of an old sack and left-over scraps her mother had painstakingly sewn together. She reached deep into her skirt pocket and pulled out the doll, its dress tattered and one button eye missing, its sewn mouth stitched in a frayed half-smile. It still smelled of perfume, or maybe that was just a memory. She'd kept that doll, clinging to the comfort it gave, because it had come from her mother and because it made her just a bit less the tomboy Cyrus had raised. Made her realize she was entitled to show her emotions and not hide them away; to mourn, to cry when need be. To grieve. Her father had been cold in some ways and she couldn't recall ever having seen him shed a tear, even when her mother passed on. Hell, maybe she was too, least the ways she cared to reveal to the outside world.

Although it pained her to admit it, Jim Sutter had reached something within that part of her, that part that was still a little girl clinging to a ragged doll. He had pierced the layers of fogged pain and grief, the loneliness. He had touched something inside that told her maybe she had more to live for than revenge on Stroud and the prospect of being murdered by him within the week when she refused to leave her land. Last night she hadn't cared a lick about that. Now . . . now she found she somehow wanted Jim Sutter to kill Stroud, in spite of her admonitions to the contrary where killing was concerned.

She was a hypocrite; plain and simple. But she didn't care, because someone had to pay for her father's death and maybe an eye for an eye made perfect sense. A killer for a killer . . .

No, Jim Sutter was more than that and she knew it, now. She hadn't given him a chance last night while she was so swollen with grief and outraged at life, hadn't been fair.

She turned and looked towards the

direction the manhunter had taken, gazed that way for a very long time, and a worry arose unbidden:

'Don't let him kill you, Mr Sutter . . .' she whispered, not sure why she cared.

Then she turned, mouthing a small prayer for her father, and wandered in the direction of the empty house.

* * *

The Stark Bar S compound spread out as far as the eye could see. Its terrain ran the gamut from clusters of trees and brush to lush grazeland and rolling hills dotted with longhorns.

Jim Sutter reined up near the compound, which was built in a roughly circular pattern hundreds of yards in diameter. He saw a sprawling bunkhouse and scattered outbuildings — an ice-house, barns and stables, corrals and storage sheds. Cowhands bustled about, tending to chores and repairs and the everyday drudgery of running a large ranch. The spread was immense, sprawling this way and that, and Jim wondered why a man with so much was so intent on gathering up more. He should have counted his blessings and been satisfied with his fortune, but that wasn't the case. He murdered to acquire more, crushed small-timers to gain what he considered his rightful lot.

Jim urged his bay forward, keeping a sharp eye out for any sign of Stroud or opposition. As he rode in, a few hands glanced his way, but none made an effort to stop him, which was a mite strange in itself. He figured a man like Stark would have made enough enemies to post guards and enforcers. That he didn't indicated the man was either stupid or imbued with such brash cockiness he figured no one dared touch him.

Jim wondered if Stroud was close by and tensed, knowing if he made another mistake it would likely be his last. His gaze roved but he spotted no sign of the mankiller, no indication the Bar S was anything more than a typical cattle spread. Still, he felt hidden eyes on him, somewhere. Stark was letting him approach, that he felt sure of, was letting him play his hand, determining just what Jim intended before taking action.

The ranch house itself was huge and sprawled for hundreds of feet of freshly painted adobe with beams of hand-split cedar for the roof and a veranda stretching from end to end. The door looked strong enough for a fortress and window openings were two feet thick.

He reached the veranda and reined up. Stepping from the saddle, keeping a watch on his back this time, he made his way towards the door. It opened as he approached, confirming his suspicion that Stark had seen him coming. A manservant stood in the entry way, looking him over, then ushered him in without even asking his business. Jim felt vaguely comforted he was allowed to keep his Peacemaker.

The fact also gave him a quiver of unease; it meant Stark did not feel threatened by him in any way and likely the gun would be of little use.

Stroud. The manhunter had to be close by. That was why Stark felt so confident.

He was conducted into an elaborately decorated parlour with a high ceiling. The room held expensive furniture, rich mahogany tables with cabriole legs and ball and claw feet imported from the East, plush chairs with luxurious upholstery. French paintings adorned the freshly painted walls and a chandelier hung from the ceiling. An ornate black safe with gold trim sat flush against the south side. Jim passingly studied the safe, wondering if it held a certain land title.

'Mr Sutter . . . ' a voice said and his gaze went to the large windows, in front of which stood a man, a man who commanded a presence totally the opposite of Vinton Stroud. Where Stroud was dark and threatening this man was coated with a false front of dignity that only came to men with too much self-importance. He was soft around the middle and his jowly face was blocky at the jaw. His hairline had receded nearly to the middle of his skull. His small eyes rested in deep pits; they constantly darted in their sockets, giving the fella a shifty-eyed look that would have made him a horrible poker player but an excellent huckster. His vested suit was tailored, a dove-coloured shirt with royal-blue tie completing the arrangement, but the rich material and fine cut made no difference in its ill fit. It bulged at the waist and hung loose as a turkey's wattle at the shoulders.

'You know who I am?' Jim wasn't surprised by the fact. He knew Stroud would fill Stark in on any potential opposition.

The man laughed with all the sincerity of a wooden nickel. 'Of course. I know everyone and everything that goes on in Holliday, especially matters that may require my attention.'

'You mean matters that might get in your way.' Jim felt no intimidation where Rutherford Stark was concerned. Stark was only dangerous in a round-about sense; the man would not threaten Jim with gunplay or fists. He would get someone else to do his dirty work. Upfront there was only the unctuous manner, the game of feint and parry.

Stark smiled, the expression a masterpiece of condescension. 'Call it what you will, Mr Sutter. I call it good business. But let me come right to the point: why have you come here? Surely a man such as yourself has no business with me when not summoned.'

Jim let a small smile filter onto his lips. 'I don't hire out to men like you, Stark. Only legit ranchers.'

Stark's gaze washed cold. 'And what, pray tell, makes you decide I am not legit, as you say?'

Since Stark had not pulled punches Jim decided to return the courtesy. 'You hired a man named Vinton Stroud to kill Cyrus Pendelton when he wouldn't sell his land to you outright.'

Jim studied the man, looking for any sign of guilt or fury, but Stark only gave an irritated laugh, doing a remarkable job at keeping his face straight.

'Vinton Stroud is my cousin. He is here for a well-deserved rest. The man is a legend, you know. He's done more for the West than any single man ever has. You should kiss his boots, Mr Sutter. He broke the trail for your type.'

Jim uttered a scoffing laugh. 'Trail he broke was cut way before he stepped foot on this land.'

'How so, sir?' Stark's mouth took an arrogant turn. Jim felt like putting a fist down the cattleman's throat.

'He's a murderer, plain and simple. He ain't the first and maybe not even the worst, but that don't make a difference. He ain't ridin' with all his gear. He kills for pleasure.'

Stark raised an eyebrow. 'As opposed to what — duty? Some misguided sense of what's right and what's wrong?'

'You might say as much. Every profession has a code, even manhuntin', and I reckon he never has abided by it.'

'Oh, come now, Mr Sutter. You're an idealist, an anachronism. Look around, look at the West and how it's growing. It's nourished by blood, Mr Sutter. The weak perish while the strong flourish and rightly so. There is no right and wrong, only progress and gain.'

'As long as that gain goes into your coffers?'

Stark grinned. 'Well, it's got to go somewhere, doesn't it? Might as well find its way to me.'

'You're no better than Stroud, Mr Stark. Just more greedy and underhanded. You're an accessory to murder as well as a cowardly sonofabitch.'

The grin dropped from his face and his small eyes went dark with fury. 'What the devil gives you the right to come into my home and accuse me of such nonsense, Sutter?' His tone was indignant, pregnant with bravado.

Jim held his ground. 'Like I said, you had Stroud kill Cyrus Pendelton for his land and now you're threatenin' his daughter.'

Stark struggled to put on a false front but was plainly annoyed. He was not used to having men challenge his authority or word. 'Oh, come now, Sutter, why would I bother having Pendelton killed? I will take his land legally sooner or later. He was an old man. All I had to do was wait him out.'

'I might have thought that, too, Mr Stark, 'cept from what I heard I reckon you don't take no too well. I got a notion you decided to make an example out of him in case some other locals got a notion to resist your expansion?'

Stark's face flickered with something and Jim reckoned he had hit the peg on the head. Stark simply stood for no opposition and dealt harshly with any slight, perceived or otherwise. And he wouldn't tolerate any dissension getting a chance to spread.

Stark cleared his throat, a flush of red tinting his features, jowls quaking. 'I assure you, Mr Sutter, I do not know what you are talking about. You are wasting your time and mine coming here. You may leave now.' The tone dismissed him flatly. The manservant seemed to appear from nowhere but Jim knew the fellow must have been lurking close by the entire time. His gaze locked on the man with a steady accusative glare.

'You call Stroud off Ruby Pendelton or you'll regret it.'

Stark cocked an eyebrow. 'Are you threatening me, Mr Sutter?'

'You bet I am.'

Stark laughed, a response Jim would not have expected. Anger, indignation, anything else, maybe. 'Mr Sutter, if what you say about me is true, that I detest being said no to and had a part in the death of Cyrus Pendelton, then surely you must realize that any threat directed at me would likely be in poor judgement?'

Jim nodded. 'You're right about one thing, Stark, it is a judgement call. But I reckon Stroud already knows my intent and that makes a threat towards you little more than salt in an open wound.'

'Man like you has his uses, Mr Sutter. Sure your loyalty can't be bought? Find most manhunters have their price. I could make it worth your while.'

A look of surprise crossed Jim's face. 'Why, Mr Stark, you truly amaze me. I waltz in here accusin' you of murder and avarice and you offer me a job. You lookin' to keep your enemies close enough to kill?' Jim put as much sarcasm into it as he could.

Stark reddened and turned towards the window. 'Make no mistake about it, Mr Sutter, you are the enemy if you refuse my offer. The proposition is sincere. A man of power needs the skills your kind offers. But I demand total allegiance.'

'Don't reckon allegiance is at the top of Stroud's list. He's as like to turn on you as he is work for you.'

Stark's bulky frame took on a rigidness and Jim knew the thought had crossed the cattleman's mind more than once.

'Last chance, Mr Sutter.' His voice lowered.

'No, Mr Stark. Never. Not for all the blood money you could offer me.'

'Suit yourself, Mr Sutter. Good day . . . ' The cattle baron's tone was filled with icy intent and confirmed the notion Stark was not a man to say no to. Jim turned and walked from the house, figuring he had poked at a rattlesnake too many times for it not to try biting.

★　★　★

'You'd best been listening,' said Rutherford Stark, turning from the window as Vinton Stroud came into the parlour. A bemused expression played across the mankiller's features. He twisted the end of his mustache.

'I hope that tone was meant for Sutter and not me.' Stroud's eyes glinted with intent. He saw Stark go rigid and take a step back. His cousin was afraid of him, in spite of the bluster, and Stroud enjoyed that. Stark might have thought he hired him but Vinton Stroud wasn't a man who took orders if he chose not to. He did his job, as long as it suited him and that was that. As Stroud took a step towards Stark, a nervous jitter danced in the cattleman's small eyes. His cousin was a blithering coward at heart, greedy for power to make up for his lack of spine, but he failed to realize one thing: true power didn't come from lily-livered ambition that removed obstacles from a path, it came from force and iron nerve that went right through them.

'Yeah, yeah it was. I should have killed him where he stood.'

Stroud bellowed a laugh and Stark's features pinched with insult. 'Hell, cousin, we both know you never were one to get your hands dirty. That's why you hired me. 'Sides, he's more than you can handle.'

'Hell he is!' Stark shouted with a bravado Vinton saw through instantly. Fury seethed behind the cattleman's small eyes. The reaction amused him and as long as it did his cousin went on living.

Stroud strode deeper into the room, glanced out through the window at the retreating form of Jim Sutter. 'I had the drop on him earlier today. That fella had no fear in his eyes, unlike you, my dear cousin. Ain't many men who can look me in the eye without turnin' yella. Not that man. He's got sand.' Stroud paused, mind wandering. 'No fear, just questions, but them questions are his weakness. Every man's got one, Stark.' Stroud turned back to him. 'You just got more than your share.'

Stark's face went from red to purple. Stroud knew the cattleman would be infuriated at any aspersions cast in the direction of his character and sovereignty. He also knew there wasn't a damn thing his cousin would do about it.

Stark went to a table and poured himself a drink from a crystal decanter. He swallowed a huge gulp and some of the fury drained from his attitude, replaced by a sly look Stroud didn't care for. 'Every man has a weakness, Stroud? What about you? I don't see any.'

A pitiful attempt to gain an edge and Stroud damn near laughed aloud. 'And you won't.'

Stark's eyes hardened. 'I want him dead.'

Stroud gave the cattleman a humourless smile. 'This ain't an old man you got a grudge against, Stark.'

'What's the difference? No one turns me down. No one.'

Stroud peered at the jowly man with a look of challenge and mild contempt. 'That so?'

Stark squirmed under that gaze. 'No,' he said meekly.

'You best hope I don't get a notion to

test that . . . ' Stroud turned back to the window. 'As far as Mr Sutter goes, well, all in good time, Stark. All in good time. Right now the beautiful lost Lenore demands my favours . . . '

Stark looked at him, perplexed. 'Who?'

Stroud chuckled. 'That bar whore who stole you blind and sent your oats backwards.'

'Her name's Camilla.'

'What's in a name long as it ends up on a tombstone?'

'Just see to it she's taken care of.'

'Consider the job done.' Stroud turned and brushed past the portly cattleman. He could feel Stark staring after him and wondered how long it would be before his gun had a bullet with his cousin's name on it.

6

Camilla Espita was sick and tired of usin' her backside to get what she wanted out of life. She folded her arms as she looked out over the bar-room, the Durham and sour booze smell cloying in her nostrils and melancholy washing over what was left of her soul.

She'd wandered from saloon to saloon since she was barely thirteen when her first fella, a cousin and smelly sonofabitch, she recollected, had sent her purity whistlin' to the west wind. She had a knack for hornswogglin' menfolk, that was sure, a knack for whisperin' sweet nothin's just as buttery as could be to fellas too drunk to know the difference 'tween lies and cowflop. Cowboys told her she had the lips of an angel and a body moulded by the Devil hisself. That didn't change things a lick though.

Lately she felt tired, worn. Fed up to high falutin' hell with saloon life, weary of fellas who stank of cow dung and sweat and thought they could do whatever the diddly damn they wanted to her for two bits a pleasure. Hell of a way to make a livin', she reckoned but what else was she good at?

'Cept stealin'. Oh, yes, she had a practised hand at that and could filch a man's britches right from under his saddle as pretty as she pleased. And steal she did, the way her womanhood had been stolen from her.

She wondered about that fella a few weeks back, though, that cattleman she had tried to hornswoggle out of his wick-dippin'. Something about that scalawag wasn't quite right and she had reckoned he was a good deal more liquored up than he was when she pretended to light his lamp. She never thought there was a chance in hog hell he'd discover she was duping him. It was a trick she had pulled on countless cowhands and miners; she'd learned early on a woman with a pair of strong thigh muscles could beguile a fella into believin' a woman's heaven was somewhere south of where it was s'posed to be. This was the first time she could recollect it failing. He had turned one of her eyes black, thrown her on the bed and taken his due anyway. She had misjudged Stark, pegging him for just another soft-around-the-middle-and-between-the-ears cattle owner. He'd been downright peeled about it, too.

So had she. After he had fallen into a noisy sleep she had gotten even by lifting his thick roll of greenbacks and some fine kitchen silver on her way out of his ranch.

For days she looked over her shoulder, figuring he would track her down and demand the money and possessions back. She would have ridden out of Holliday right after leavin' the ranch if had it not been for the easy access to laudanum the doc provided. Stark's greenbacks and silver would pay for a goodly measure of that.

She'd felt surprised when Stark hadn't come after her. She'd pegged him for a yellowback who'd want to get even in some way and again she reckoned she'd made an error in judgement. He was just lily-livered, brave when it came to gettin' a gal alone and knocking her brains out, but that was it. She figured he'd not want his men to know a bar gal had gotten the better of him and counted his losses.

Camilla sighed and pulled a brown bottle from her bodice top, taking a swig of the fiery liquid within. The narcotic slid smoothly down her throat. A bit of the depression lifted and her head started to dance a warm dance. Wiping her lips on her forearm, she uttered a curse and spat on the sawdust-covered floorboards. Even laudanum didn't bring the pleasure it once had. It was getting harder to feel the drug's effects, taking larger amounts to hide the fact she was what she was and it was a hell of a thing to be.

Disgusted, she tucked the bottle back into her sateen top and staggered for the stairs that led to the upper level.

She stumbled on the first step. Gripping the rail, feeling nausea churn her belly, she wondered if she were going to throw up again. She'd been getting sick often since that Stark fella took his way and she reckoned that was a piss poor sign.

The upper hallway shimmered with cidery light from wall lanterns, their glow washing across red *fleur-de-lis* wallpaper. She paused, shivering, absently fingering a cameo brooch on her bodice. An odd premonition of dread wandered through her and she wondered what the hell it could be.

That man . . .

Yes, the fella from last night. Another shiver rattled her at the memory of those black eyes. What had he wanted? Who was he? He had called her something. What was it?

Lenore. That was it. Maybe he had her confused with someone else.

Maybe, but she didn't think so. She hadn't cared for the look she had seen in his eyes. He was loco as an ass-bit dog.

Shuddering, she stumbled to the door to her room. As she paused in front of it, she recollected how his eyes had cut into her. She rubbed at the spot on her wrist where his grip had left welts. She prayed she never saw that sidewinder again.

That was why she had come up early tonight: to avoid him. She pushed open the door and staggered into the dark room, going to the bedstand and fumbling for a lucifer. The match flared and she lit the kerosene lamp. She stared, transfixed, into the jittering flame as she held the glass chimney. Another chill went through her as an image of the man's face seemed to rise in the flame, wavering, dark eyes damning her.

If that fella came back . . .

A sound.

She jolted, a wave of coldness

washing through her. Her heart started to thud and filled her throat.

A sound. A creak, drawn out and followed by a small click. She recognized it and it gave her a sensation of frozen panic.

For it was the sound of the door swinging shut, the latch engaging. She turned slowly, to see a dark figure, back pressed against the wall, palm flat against the door, fingers splayed after swinging it shut. She shuddered, realizing he had been behind the door the entire time, waiting for her.

A gasp escaped her lips and the chimney dropped from numbed fingers. It shattered with a sound like a gunshot, glass spewing across the floorboards.

The sallow lantern glow made the man look hideous, demonic, somehow, like a yellowed skull with a soup-strainer mustache. The man from the night before.

'Lenore . . . ' he whispered, stepping away from the wall.

'I ain't your goddamn Lenore, cowboy.' Her voice came as if from a distance and held little conviction.

' 'Come!' ' His voice snapped out and Camilla froze with panic. ' 'Let the burial rite be read — the funeral song be sung! — An anthem for the queenliest dead that ever . . . died . . . so . . . young — ' '

'Jesus H Christamighty, you're plumb outta your saddle — ' Her hand darted to her bodice top and this time she yanked out an Over-and-Under. She tried to aim the .41 and jerk the trigger, but her hand quaked too violently.

The man's hand seemed to move faster than her eye could follow and she was suddenly staring down the barrel of a black Peacemaker.

A prayer died on her lips as a bullet punched into her brain.

*　*　*

Jim opened the office door and the marshal looked up from behind the desk. A frown turned his lips.

'Nice to see you're still alive.' His uncle sounded as if he were only half-joking.

'Not so sure I am. Got a headache big as New Mex.' He lowered himself into the hard-backed chair and tossed the telegraph slips onto the desk.

'What the hell happened? You look like hell warmed over.'

Jim ran a finger over his swollen lips. 'Got kicked by a mule.'

'A mule named Stroud, no doubt.' A glint of anger mixed with relief flashed in Glover's eyes. 'You're damn lucky you ain't dead. Anything I can pin him down on?'

'Nothin' you could hold him long for. You arrest him you want to make sure it's a hangin' offence.'

The marshal gave a reluctant nod. 'Reckon you're right. What're these?' He gathered up the telegraph slips and shuffled through them.

'Those are the reason Stroud pistol-whipped me. I did a bit of checking on him and Stark through a Pinkerton friend. Stroud didn't care for it. Told me not to help Pendelton's daughter out in no uncertain terms, either. He's crazy as they come. And you're right, he enjoys killin' too much. It's some kind of opiate to him.'

The marshal nodded, studying the slips. 'Like I expected. Nothing on Stark, I see . . . '

'No, but plenty on Stroud. Ain't quite the hero we thought. Appears he's been implicated in a number of killin's over minor issues, certainly nothing worthy of a fella with his reputation.'

Glover frowned. 'Shot a man for stealin' a can of beans from a general store in Catero, another for accidentally courtin' another fella's wife in Mascarada . . . '

'List goes on and on, nothin' worth even jailin' a man for in some cases. Just nuisance stuff mostly, though in each incident he claimed self-defence and folks were either too scared or too dead to say different. He's gone bad, no two ways about it.'

The marshal looked up. 'He's gone worse . . . '

'Has a habit of disappearin' for long spells, too. No one really knows where.'

'Then we're right back where we started, with nothin' legal to hang him on.'

'Reckon that might not be long in comin'.'

Marshal Glover cocked an eyebrow. 'What do you mean?'

'I had myself a parley with Rutherford Stark today.'

'You what?' The marshal's jaw dropped.

'Rode out to his ranch after tellin' Ruby Pendelton I was aimin' to help.'

'There's goddamn healthier things to do, son. You should have let me question Stark.'

'Reckon after that encounter with Stroud, Holliday ain't the best place for my health anyway.'

'How did Stark take it?'

''Bout like you'd expect. Plenty of

bluster and lots of denial.' Jim shrugged. 'All in all, can't say I got anything more than I already suspected. But I did turn him down for a job offer.'

'Man's got *bolas*. I'll say that for him.'

'And he's got Stroud. He figures he can do anything he wants long as that's in his favour.'

Marshal Glover's frown deepened. 'You're like to get your brains shot out crossin' Stark.'

'I put him on notice and said no plain as day to him. If he's what we think he is I reckon that'll force him into a move sooner rather than later and that's what we want.'

'Do we?' A spark of fear showed in the marshal's eyes.

'Sure of it, Uncle Frank. We gotta catch him and Stroud crossin' the line 'fore we can hang them.'

The door burst open and both men looked towards it. A girl in a purple sateen bodice stumbled in, her coral-daubed face turned with fear. Jim stood.

'Marshal!' she said, gasping. 'You best come quick!'

'What happened, Justine?' The lawdog went to her and gripped her shoulders, steadying her.

'It's Camilla, Marshal. She done got her ticket punched.'

'She's dead?' Jim's gaze travelled past the dove, across the darkened street to the saloon.

'Ain't never seen her no deader!'

The marshal released the dove and grabbed his hat, setting it atop his head. He stepped past the frightened bar girl, headed for the saloon. Jim followed, a sinking feeling in his belly.

Everything was quiet in the Silver Spur as they entered and Stroud sat relaxed in a chair, staring at them, a vacant look on his features. He lifted a glass of whiskey to his lips and took a slug. After setting the glass back on the table, the mankiller picked up a book and tucked it in his pocket. Jim couldn't see the title, but he felt mild surprise; Stroud didn't seem like the reading type.

The marshal glanced towards the stairs, back to Stroud. 'You're responsible for this, I s'pose?'

Stroud gave him a smile and gave Jim a curt nod of acknowledgement. 'Reckon I am. She drew on me, Marshal. Gave me no choice but to defend myself.'

Marshal Glover's brow knotted. 'Seems a mite convenient, two nights in a row . . . '

Stroud shrugged. 'I can't change circumstances, Marshal. I merely defended myself. She got what she had comin'.' His voice held an utter lack of regret or remorse.

The marshal let out a disgusted sigh and drilled Stroud with his gaze. 'Don't you go nowhere.' He glanced at Jim then went towards the stairs. Jim followed a beat behind, noticing the shootist never took his gaze off them as they went up.

Reaching the room, the marshal knelt and looked over the body of Camilla Espita, who, as Justine had said, had never been no deader. A gaping gory hole shown in her forehead and half her brains had come out the back of her skull and splattered across the floor and bed.

Jim turned away. The sight of death was one he would never get used to, especially in such a grisly manner.

'She's got an Over-and-Under clutched in her hand,' the marshal said finally. 'Reckon we got another case of nothin' to hold him on.'

Jim nodded, as the marshal stood. 'This was the girl he had last night.'

'Yep, sure is.'

'Reckon she was in more danger than we thought.' He felt a surge of guilt. Perhaps if they had taken Stroud's actions last night more serious this wouldn't have happened, but it was hard to predict what a man like that would do, or why. He had some reason for wanting the dove dead, or Stark did, and tonight, Jim felt sure, the shootist had carried out no less than an execution. She would have had no chance against Stroud and the killer had known it. For Camilla Espita Jim said a silent prayer.

'Not a hell of a lot we can do to right that.'

'Not tonight anyway.'

They went back downstairs and Stroud stood, eyeing Jim first, then the marshal.

'Much as it galls me, you're free to go, Stroud.' Glover didn't hide the disgust in his voice.

Stroud grinned and set his hat atop his head. 'I take the notion you ain't happy about that, lawdog.'

Glover's eyes narrowed and locked with the mankiller's. Jim saw no fear in his uncle's demeanour this time. 'You're dead right there, Stroud. I think you're a damned butcher. I had my druthers you'd be hangin' from a rope while I sold tickets and danced a jig.'

Stroud's expression darkened. 'Best

watch your talk, Marshal.'

'How's that, Mr Stroud? Keep in mind I ain't one of your gamblers or whores or seventy-year-old men.'

Stroud's eyes flickered with a look Jim didn't care for and he saw grim determination on his uncle's face. The lawman had decided to take a stand, fear be damned. Jim suddenly wished he hadn't.

'What crimes have you got, Marshal?' Stroud didn't wait for a reply. He brushed past them and out through the batwings, leaving only cold silence behind.

★　★　★

The bloated October moon stood high in the star-sprinkled velvet of the night sky, throwing an alabaster white-wash over the abandoned mining town of Eldorado. Once a booming settlement where men in frock coats travelled from the East and prospectors and their families came from every direction to stake a claim on silver, now it had fallen to ruin and the haunting echoes of all who had traded their lives for the false promise of riches and never-realized dreams. Buildings were collapsing, roofs rotting, doors ajar. Awnings hung askew and windows were cracked or simply jagged pieces of glass in empty frames. Tumbleweeds skittered along the sagging boardwalks. With a thin skritching noise something slithered over the dust in the darkness. Damn little resided in Eldorado, except for ghosts, rattlesnakes and scorpions.

And Vinton Stroud.

The manhunter took a strange comfort here, a sense of kinship with the town he had staked claim on. Something about its eerie lonesomeness, its lost hope, made him feel welcomed, at peace, at least as much as a man like him could.

The speculated lode silver had turned out to be little more than a few impotent veins, amounting to no more than disappointment and shattered souls and the yellowing buzzard-picked bones of those who risked life and livelihood on empty dreams. Vinton Stroud saw the appropriateness in that. He had dreamt once, of holding forth those ideals that Sutter fella still carried, of making a difference and saving the West from itself, but time and reality had shown him what a fool's mission that was, and now those dreams were dust, like this town.

Eldorado.

A gallant Knight.

Fallen into disrepair and abandonment.

Like his dreams.

Like his soul.

Hell of a thing.

He rode slowly through the town, ribbons of moonlight slashing across the boardwalks and wide rutted main street. If he looked carefully he could still pick out the dark blotches of old blood staining the boards where men had shot one another over disputed claims or false affronts.

He let out a humourless laugh; the sound died in eerie echoes. There was a time he might have admired Sutter, embraced his ideals. No longer. Now the man was merely an opportunity for challenge, a chance to make the intensity of killing more acute and pure. The bar dove tonight had provided damn little of that. In fact he had felt strangely numbed afterward, cheated.

Stroud came from his woolgathering and slowed his horse as he approached the junction of the ghost town, his gaze lifting to the structure that squatted in the moonlight like an insane goblin welcoming him home.

His Usher. His creation, constructed with the blood and toil of the various men he had hired to build it then murdered and buried on the grounds or within its walls.

A house, or more rightly an extension of what he had become, of the dreams that had bled into nightmares.

Frosted with moonlight it reared up in magnificent yet disturbingly sinister contour. The dwelling was an incredible mismatch of architectural styles and materials. An aesthetic nightmare, parts seemed jammed together with no particular attention to grace or line or forethought of conception. It meandered this way and that, an array of weird jutting angles and rounded abutments crazily stitched together. One section was fashioned of logs chinked with manure, while directly attached came another portion constructed of sawn lumber. Adobe took over after that, hand-peeled poles set close together, walls three-feet thick with deep-set windows. Parts were painted white, while other areas were brown or tinted red. Horizontal shiplap siding gave way to vertical plank-and-board, adjoined like a designer's argument. The pitch of the roof varied from flat to steep and everything in between, materials ranging from hand-hewn beams to hand-cut cedar shingles to sod, even tin. Other parts were gabled in Gothic Revival style, wood frame construction beneath, board and batten siding with arched windows and doors. Eastlake styling took over as the house angled diagonally backwards, complete with latticework, cut-outs and rows of spindles and knobs in an asymmetrical nightmare; windows were double-hung sash — twelve panes of glass, six in the upper part, six in the lower — clapboard siding painted white. Jutting frontwise and left from that style came an area of abode sporting a veranda that abruptly gave way to dusty ground.

Vinton Stroud stared in admiration at the homestead that had taken years to construct. He'd filtered a goodly part of his earnings into it, which was part of the reason he accepted the funds from men like his cousin. His usher, indeed.

He drew up before the sprawling beast of a house and dismounted, tethering his sorrel to a hitch post and stepping up onto a wooden porch that led to a Gothic Revival doorway. His boots made eerie clomping echoes.

Entering the structure, he paused in an ante-room, which was completely bare except for a small metal tube covered by a thin screen extending from the wall close to the ceiling. A short hall zigzagged at contrary angles from its right side. He took careful steps, avoiding certain areas of floor, making his way deeper in to the interior of the residence. The inside showed just as much a hodgepodge of styles and contrasts as the outside: puncheon floors gave way to imported tile, to polished hardwood to even areas of hard pack. Adobe walls were tinted red, window frames and doors painted blue. Halls led nowhere, simply ending in doors that didn't open or opened to walls of brick.

He came through a small parlour whose walls shown in opposing colours and embellishment, green and orange on adjoining ones, blue-flowered wallpaper on another. Some rooms held no furniture while others held too much. As with the house, the furniture was a mismatch of styles, dating and elegance. The parlour held a horse-hair stuffed chair; a sofa of carved rosewood and rich upholstery; tables with turned legs carved with Acanthus leaf motif, heavily scrolled ball feet and cherry wood American Empire styling from forty years past; a spindle-back Boston rocker with cyma-curved arms and seat, stencilled with gilt and coloured designs; and a circular sofa with a centre column backrest filled one corner. One wall held Currier and Ives Prints hung directly beside daguerreotypes of himself. Wall sconces held candles while still others sported lanterns.

He took careful steps, avoiding a certain spot on the oriental carpet and entered a corridor with a stairway without a rail that jutted directly out of a wall. An iron tier chandelier hung to its left; a sloping hallway led beneath the upper level flooring. He went up the stairs slowly, avoiding the top step and opening a door at the top that had a glass knob. The opening led into a long hall of closed doors. Lanterns burned with buttery light on dingy papered walls, giving the corridor a funereal atmosphere. Most of the doorways opened to bricked-up rooms containing the rotting corpses or yellowed bones of those unlucky enough to have crossed his bad side; others were ornamental and didn't open at all.

He paused at one door, then threw it open and entered a darkened room. Ribbons of moonlight, slicing through the barred window, fell across the floor in weird twisting patterns.

Going to a table, he struck a lucifer and lit a kerosene lantern, turning the flame high. The light threw jittering yellow ghosts across the walls and sent shadows cowering.

The room was sparsely furnished, besides the rickety table there was only a hard-backed chair. The barred window on the far wall looked out over a dusty courtyard. In a corner to the left of the doorway lay a pile of random objects, watches, bandannas, belt buckles and holsters, rings and vest buttons, spurs and hair combs that rose nearly four feet high. Mementoes of the blood he had spilled.

Reaching into a pocket he pulled out a small cameo brooch he had taken off the whore he'd shot tonight and tossed it into the pile. It landed next to the watch he had taken from Cyrus Pendelton.

Above the door, on an inset shelf, sat a statue of a black bird, its glossy onyx eyes seeming to stare down at him condemningly. Some day soon he reckoned he would blow that bird straight to hell. The more he looked at it the more he detested it.

' 'Deep into that darkness peering . . . ' ' The words came out in a whisper.

A sudden throbbing arose in his skull. Indistinct and muffled at first, it crescendoed until it became a pounding heartbeat.

Louder, more intense with every passing second. Maddening. He pressed his hands to his ears, trying to crush the sound from his mind but it continued to rise.

Tap-tap-tapping . . .

Ungently rapping . . .

Pain. Knives of agony stabbed through his brain. Sweat broke out on his brow and streamed down his face.

' 'Deep into . . . ' ' His voice was a harsh grating whisper.

His vision blurred. Onerous grey shapes, their forms indistinct and ghostly, gibbering, began to skitter at the edge of his sight.

' 'Deep into that darkness peering . . . deep into that . . . darkness . . . ' '

The throbbing heartbeat in his mind grew louder louder, louder, pounding from the deep recesses of his brain, threatening to burst his skull.

He groaned, his lips moving with sibilant words. ' ' . . . Darkness peering . . . long I stood, wondering, fearing . . . ' '

172

The words turned into a scream of agony. He staggered about, hands still pressed against his ears. The shapes at the edges of his vision whirled and darted, growing distinct with the terrified faces of the men he had murdered. They pointed accusing fingers, damning him, their hollow sunken eyes pleading for the mercy that never came.

' 'Long . . . long I stood!' ' he yelled, pain staggering him. ' ' . . . Wondering, fearing!' '

The heartbeat.

Tap-tap-tapping . . .

Ungently rapping . . .

Louder, louder, shattering, consuming. The ghosts of the murdered closed in from every angle, brushing him with their burning torches.

Agony. Lancing his skull. Sharper with each thrust.

His hands trembled as he pulled them away from his ears. He fell against a wall, groaning.

The heartbeat, louder still. The

ghosts, closer always.

Deep into that darkness peering . . .

His hands dropped, slowly, every inch an effort gained by extreme power of will. Sweat streaked down his face and his eyelids fluttered, as another spoke of torment drove through his brain.

The Peacemaker.

The Devil's Peacemaker.

His trembling fingers closed over its ornately carved handle. He pried it from its holster, its weight exaggerated, so he could barely lift it.

Long I stood there wondering, fearing . . .

He cleared leather in a final explosive moment and shrieked.

'Noooo! I won't . . . let . . . you take me!'

Tap-tap-tapping . . .

Ungently rapping . . .

He jerked the trigger and the roar of the Peacemaker thundered over the horrendous thrumming of heartbeats and ghostly gibbering. Strength flooded back into him and he swept his aim about the room, squeezing the trigger over and over. Glass blew out of the window, exploding into shards that glittered with captured moonlight as they rained onto the dusty courtyard below, like dying fireflies.

Plaster erupted from walls in powdery chunks as lead punched deep. Acrid blue smoke singed his nostrils.

The ghosts dissolved under the leaden barrage and the heartbeats diminished, fading. Into nothingness.

'Goddamn . . . ' he muttered, dropping to his knees as the strength left his legs. He knelt there gasping, sweat trickling off his chin, staring at the Peacemaker, his salvation, his deliverer. His hand quaked, palms slick with sweat. His vision focused, the agony in his skull a memory now.

Deep into that darkness peering, long I stood there wondering, fearing . . .

The intensity of the attacks, those forced looks into that darkness, were increasing. This had been the worst yet.

Each time it was harder to hold the ghosts off. They came when they wanted and some day he knew they would overcome him.

But not today. And not tomorrow. And not until the thrill of killing had been satiated.

'I am Vinton Stroud!' he screamed. He slammed a fist against the floor.

'I . . . am . . . Vinton . . . Stroud!' He reared up and swung the Peacemaker towards the statue above the door and pulled the trigger a final time. The ebony bird shattered into fragments and Vinton Stroud began to laugh uncontrollably.

7

'And so from the dust which we came we return . . . '

The preacher's words echoed sombre and final in the late afternoon air. Droplets of rain fell from a sky covered with gunmetal-coloured clouds, spattering the dirt piled beside the open grave. The boneyard was small, surrounded by a rusting iron fence. As the preacher concluded the ceremony, he offered comforting words to Ruby, who stood silent and stolid at the graveside. She wore a simple black dress and her hair was pulled tightly back. No tears came, but her lips, held in a hard line, quivered occasionally.

She knelt and scooped up a handful of soil, saying some small prayer Jim couldn't hear then letting the dirt trickle through her fingers into the grave.

As the preacher departed, a gravedigger began to shovel dirt into the hole. Jim saw her nearly lose control then. She turned away, a shudder rattling her frame.

'Never did cotton to funerals,' said the marshal, starting forward. Jim stopped him.

'Let me talk to her. Least I can do.'

The marshal peered at him, nodded. 'Do somethin' for her, son. I hate to see a spirited woman like that at the mercy of her grief.' Glover set his hat on his head and walked away from the boneyard. Jim waited until she was ready to turn and face him.

A jagged streak of lightning sizzled across the sky, followed by a crash of thunder. Gunmetal clouds darkened to charcoal and a chilly wind swept through the cemetery. The greyness of the afternoon penetrated to his very soul. He recollected the loss he experienced the day his parents were buried. He recalled crying as only a child can cry, then crying no more and just shutting himself off, not speaking for days, until his uncle came for him.

'Mister Sutter . . . ' Her words were soft and heavy with sorrow. Coming from his thoughts, he saw her standing before him, a tear tracing a path down her cheek. He knew she no longer hated him. In her eyes was a plea to take away some of the awful pain, to console her the way no one or nothing else could. He suddenly felt sorely inadequate for the task.

'I'm sorry, ma'am . . . I know it ain't easy.'

She tried a smile that didn't work. 'Thank you kindly, Mr Sutter.' She went past and he held the iron gate open for her.

'Ma'am, where's your horse?'

'I . . . walked here. I needed to.'

'Pardon my boldness, but you look like you can barely hold yourself up.'

'I haven't slept for a couple days. I reckon that's it.' She looked at him and the sorrow in her eyes cut deep.

'When's the last time you ate, Miss Pendelton?'

'Please . . . my name's Ruby . . . '

'Ruby.' He liked the sound of it on his lips.

'Been as long, I reckon. Don't rightly recollect.'

He sighed and untethered his horse from the rail. Climbing into the saddle, he offered her a hand, half expecting her to refuse, but she accepted the gesture, placed her hand in his. She slid into the saddle behind him and he reined around. Heading his bay towards town, he couldn't deny he liked the feeling of her holding to him, her hands clutched about his belly, her body warm and pressed close. As she lay her head against his back a warm shiver swept over him. His feelings suddenly felt jumbled, sympathy tangled with a protectiveness that was almost over-whelming, a warmth beyond anything he had ever experienced.

They reached Holliday, rain coming down harder, turning dust to mud;

muck slopped under his horse's hooves. He guided the bay up to a small eatery and dismounted, offering her help. He lifted her to the boardwalk to prevent her shoes from getting caked with mud.

The eatery held a half dozen tables covered with blue-checked cloth and the scents of Arbuckle's, fresh apple pie and sizzling beefsteak filled the air. They took a table near the window and he ordered them beefstew, fresh sourdough biscuits and strong coffee.

She stared out the window into the darkening day. 'I'll miss him, Mr Sutter . . .'

'Reckon that's somethin' that won't get any easier. I still miss my parents. They were taken by sickness when I was a boy. Marshal raised me. They still cross my mind a lot, 'specially on the trail when I got too much time to think.'

'Marshal the one who taught you to do what you do?'

'Reckon you could say that. Taught

me how to shoot and track anyway. The rest was mine.'

'The rest? What is the rest, Mr Sutter?'

'Speed, experience and a kind of sixth sense manhunters develop over time, the part of me that needs to see justice done. That sense of right ain't somethin' that can be taught. Man's got it or he don't.'

'You make killin' sound so noble . . . '

Bitterness laced her words, yet he also heard something else he was not sure of. Understanding? 'I didn't mean to. Reckon it ain't noble at all, just necessary sometimes if it's on the side of law.'

A thin smile crossed her lips. 'I ain't condemnin' you any longer, Mr Sutter.' She glanced at the table and with her fork moved a piece of beef in her stew around the plate, then looked back up to him, face pinched, eyes serious. 'I've been thinkin' a lot about what you said yesterday. You're different to Stroud, ain't no doubt. But maybe I ain't so much.'

A perplexed look turned his face. 'I don't follow.'

'I don't condemn you any more because I want Stark and Stroud dead, Mr Sutter. I want them in that grave instead of my father and before they come to take what's mine. I ain't proud of it and I reckon that makes me no better than they are.'

'That's just your grief talkin', Ruby. You aren't like them a bit. Stroud is a ruthless killer and Stark . . . hell, Stark is a coward who wants power at any cost. They can't get it outright so they do it underhanded. They buy folks to do it for them.'

She studied him a moment. 'You've seen him, haven't you?'

He nodded. 'Rode out to his place yesterday. He had the balls to offer me a job workin' for him.'

She laughed but there was no humour in the expression. 'That'd be like him. He's a sonofabitch. Every time

I seen him he had someone else doin' his work for him. I don't believe a man like that has struggled for anything a day in his life.'

'Reckon you're right. I turned him down flat and, like my uncle says, he ain't a man you say no to without consequences.'

'That I am well aware of,' she said with a bitter tone. 'And in a few days he'll send that monster after me and take all I have left in the world.'

'I won't let that happen, Ruby. I swear I won't.'

'You say it with such seriousness I almost believe you. But I reckon you can't stop it. Funny thing is yesterday I wanted you to, even wanted you to kill them for me.'

'Today?'

'Today . . . ' She looked deep into his eyes and he felt a warm shiver wander through him. 'Today I don't want you to risk your life goin' after them.'

'There ain't a lot of other options. You could just leave your land and start someplace else. There's no need to face Stroud. Or you could sell to Stark.'

She gave a scoffing laugh and sat back. 'I ain't leavin' that land, Mr Sutter. My father's blood paid for it.'

'I reckon I didn't expect you to. But I also reckon you won't expect me not to be there when the time comes in that case.'

She swallowed and her eyes grew misty. 'I don't want you hurt, Jim.' His name sounded like a spring morning on her lips and he liked the way she had simply taken the right of calling him by it. 'I've seen what a man like Stroud can do.'

Jim nodded, eyes going distant a moment. 'I've seen it too, Ruby. I reckon I'll see it again, but after facing down Stark I also know I won't have much choice but to come up against him.'

She turned her head and looked out of the window. Rain streaked down in glowing rivulets: dusk had come, premature and ominous, shadows of grey sulking in corners, the pattering of water on the boardwalks and awnings droning a dismal lullaby.

Jim stood, offering his hand and helping her to her feet. 'You haven't slept in days. I'd best get you home so you can.'

'I don't know if I'll ever sleep again, least not until after Stroud comes for me.'

'If you don't, you won't be in any shape to face him.'

Her eyes met his. 'I got an extra room at the ranch. I hope it ain't improprietous of me offerin' it to you.' She smiled and a wave of warmth rushed through him. 'I don't want to be alone in that house right now. Not tonight, not this week. Beyond that — '

'Beyond that Stroud will be where he belongs, Ruby — at the end of a rope. And Stark will be there with him.'

'How can you say that?' Doubt came into her eyes. 'Stark's a powerful man and you ain't likely to pin anything on him even if . . . ' Her words trailed off.

186

'Even if Stroud doesn't kill me,' he finished.

She looked at the floor, a darkness moving across her features. He wrapped his coat around her shoulders and guided her towards the door. She put her hand in his, looked back up at him.

'You can still ride away. You don't have to risk your life for me. Stroud will come for me even if I sign away that land or pull stakes. I'd never be able to run far enough or fast enough. He's takin' Stark's direction now but a man like him don't ride second for long.'

'I'm inclined to agree 'bout that. The man's saddle ain't cinched. But I reckon you got the rest wrong, Ruby. I can't just ride away. I couldn't from the moment you came into the marshal's office.'

She gave him a warm smile that softened the lines of grief on her face, then kissed him lightly on the cheek.

As they stepped out onto the boardwalk, the rain beat cold and hard against his face. A sudden chill moved through him, bringing a sense of dread that contrasted sharply with the feelings he felt growing for the woman at his side. He tried to shrug it off, but it stayed with him. He hoped it wasn't a bad sign.

★ ★ ★

Hell, you old bastard, you never should have challenged Stroud that way . . .

Frank Glover sat behind his desk, running a finger over his upper lip and struggling to fight off the fear crawling through his innards. He stared out through the rain-streaked window into the darkening day, dread settling over him.

Stroud was guilty as hell and he knew it, but proving something was far from suspicion, and it goaded him. Goaded him enough to throw away whatever caution the years of marshallin' had taught him and issue threat to Stroud in the saloon last night and put his own life up for barter. Christamighty, he had rode Jim for doing that very thing with Stark then he had gone and stuck his own hand into the rattlesnake pit.

It was plain foolishness, instigating anything against that mankiller. He had no chance against the likes of that Stroud. But maybe he had done it for a reason. If Stroud was lookin' his way, maybe it would direct the shootist's attention away from Jim. He knew his nephew; Jim was manoeuvring Stroud and Stark's attention towards himself, setting himself up as the target instead of Ruby Pendelton. And he knew damn well why. He saw it in the boy's eyes. He was in love with that gal whether he wanted to admit it or not.

You got a bit over two months 'fore you retire . . .

Not no more, he reckoned. Not after last night. He knew damn well how a man like Vinton Stroud would respond to a challenge like the one issued. Vinton would come for him all right. It was just a matter of when.

You can't beat him . . .

Vinton Stroud was too fast, too skilled, too deadly. And Frank Glover was just an old marshal ready for pasture. He should have left that challenge to a younger man, one not bound by the law.

But could Jim beat Stroud?

The answer always came back no and Jim had pegged it when he said Frank wanted him to just ride out before it came to that. He was also right the other way: Glover wanted Jim to take Stroud down, and Stark right along with him. A hell of a contrary thing, but it was there.

'Marshal Glover . . .'

Frank Glover started, jerking from his thoughts as the voice drifted in from outside. A shiver of fear rattled his spine and for a moment he froze, hearing only the drumming dirge of the rain on the roof and the thudding cacophony of his own heart.

Godamighty . . .

It was time. Already. He had expected it but not so soon. He should have known a man like Stroud would be itching to get at him. He didn't move, a sudden surge of images whirling through his mind, scenes from his past when he had first become marshal of Holliday, when he had taught Jim to shoot and track, the many times his law had been challenged. Somehow it seemed a lot more empty than he had thought, his life. Somehow it seemed so wasted and now it was over.

It was indeed time. Time to die.

'Hell with whittlin' little wooden animals anyway . . . ' he muttered.

'Marshal Glover, I'm callin' you out.' The voice came again, the voice of the devil in a black duster who carried the instrument of eternity in the form of a Peacemaker, its handle carved with the likeness of a ram's head. 'You're a man of the law, marshal. Don't reckon you'd back down to a challenge.'

He forced himself to stand, legs wobbling. His heart filled his throat, as he walked to the rack that held his rig.

Taking down the gunbelt, he fastened it about his waist.

'I'm waitin' on ya, Marshal . . . don't make me come in there and get you. No dignity in that for a respected lawman.'

Stroud was goading him, but it made no difference. He would go out and face him, accept his challenge. Words were not needed. He had sworn an oath to uphold the law in Holliday, and that's just what he would do.

He took a breath, steeling himself against what he knew waited in the street. He looked back at his office a final time, wishing he wasn't forced to say goodbye to it this way, to a life that never was as much as he wanted it to be.

He opened the door and stepped onto the boardwalk. Rain pelted his face, icy, and a chilly autumn wind sliced right through to his soul. It all came down to a moment in a man's life, a decision made, perhaps the wrong decision in the sense where preservation was concerned, but right in another, where pride and integrity mattered. They mattered to him. Jim wasn't the only one who knew what justice was. Frank Glover knew right as well.

Marshal Glover squinted against the rain streaming down his face. The figure stood in the middle of the street, duster pulled back, the yellowed ivory handle of his Peacemaker almost glowing with demonic light from the rain and hanging lanterns' glow.

'What you want, Stroud?' Marshal Glover's voice came firm, barely. 'You got no business here.'

Stroud laughed and a jagged sizzle of lightning cut across the black clouds. Thunder shook the store fronts.

'Oh, but I do, Marshal. I'm here for you . . . '

'You got away with killin' a seventy-year-old rancher who couldn't defend himself, Stroud, but gunnin' down a marshal in cold blood for no reason is a whole 'nother thing.' He stepped off the boardwalk, moving towards the middle of the street. He must meet the mankiller there, on those terms, and have a chance, however slight, or the gunfighter would simply gun him down where he stood.

'Aidin' and abettin' a known horse stealer and land thief is as much reason as I need, Marshal. Pendelton and his daughter are guilty as old sin in my book; that makes you guilty as well.'

'Hell it does, Stroud. You're trumpin' charges and you know it. They are no more guilty than that gambler you killed or that whore you murdered, even less so.'

'Gambler cheated and the whore stole. That's good enough. See, Marshal, men like you an' that Sutter fella got the wrong notion where dispensin' justice is concerned. Justice don't belong to the righteous, it belongs to the strong, the powerful.'

'Like you and Stark . . . ' He manoeuvred to a front facing position. Fear rushed through him like a stampede but he would not back down to this man, this butcher who killed for the sheer pleasure of it.

'Like me, anyhow. Stark only thinks he's got power. He's got it as long as I say he does, though. It's time, Marshal. You know that, don't you?'

'I know it . . .'

' 'But he grew old —
This knight so bold —
And o'er his heart a shadow . . . ' '

Frank heard the words but they had no meaning to him, other than telling him Stroud was plumb out of his saddle. He said a silent prayer for Jim and blessed the Good Lord for the time he had lived and while he was at it asked for just a hair bit of the speed back he had once possessed as a younger man.

His prayer went unanswered.

His final thought was that the draw Stroud made was the fastest goddamn thing he'd ever seen. The damn black Peacemaker seemed to merely appear in Stroud's upraised hand and before he could get his own weapon fully clear of leather, flame and blue smoke erupted from the devil's gun.

Pain: not as much as he expected, for Stroud had put the bullet in a spot that would not prolong suffering. Thank the bastard for that anyway.

Frank Glover let his gun drop from nerveless fingers and clutched at the gory hole in his chest. Dropping to his knees, he pitched forward flat on his face.

*   *   *

'Whatever it takes, I'll do my best to stop him, Ruby,' said Jim, as they went across the boardwalk.

Ruby turned, hand going to his arm, stopping him, and looked into his eyes. 'I don't want you dyin', Jim. Not for me, not for anything. I reckon I don't understand some of what I'm feelin' and that first time I saw you I would have wanted nothin' better than for you and Stroud to just kill each other off. I still thought that way when you came to the ranch yesterday. But I went back to that empty house and faced the loneliness and the more I thought it over the more I realized the difference 'tween you two, and how I was no better.'

'You got every right to think that way. It don't make you as low as him, it makes you human. He don't even know the difference.'

She frowned, rain streaming down her face, off her chin. 'Reckon I ain't so sure of that. I won't let Stroud take me off my land. When he tries I'll do the very thing I damned you for, I'll put a bullet in him and probably regret it the rest of my days.'

He pulled her close, his mouth gently touching hers. She responded, and he felt hot tears mix with the rain and rush down her face. Drawing her into his arms, he held her tight as the wind and rain washed over them. Somehow he felt warm. She sobbed uncontrollably for a time, then stopped and simply held on.

Down the street . . .

His thoughts stopped dead. His eyes narrowed with hardness and a burst of fear rode through him like thunder. 'Christamighty, nooo . . . ' His voice came hard and low and Ruby pulled back, instantly aware something was dead wrong.

'Jim, what is it, what's the — '

He eased her aside and started forward but he knew he would be too late. A gunshot filled the street with thunder, echoing from the walls of buildings and through his soul. He had seen his uncle stepping into the street and the dark figure waiting there for him; he had seen Stroud's hand sweep towards his hip with a speed that was almost superhuman.

He had seen the sudden starburst of blood on his uncle's chest.

He ran towards his uncle, yelling something; he wasn't even sure what. Waves of overwhelming emotion washed over him as he watched his uncle crumple to his knees, fall forward into the mud.

He lunged into the street, heedless of the man who took a step towards his uncle and squatted over him,

Jim flung Stroud aside as the gunslinger straightened, grasping a tin star he had removed from the lawman's breast. The mankiller laughed and Jim fell to his knees, clutching at his uncle, drawing the wounded lawman's head to his chest.

Lightning sizzled across the sky. Rain streamed over him.

'Uncle Frank, please . . . '

His uncle's eyes had a glassy sheen and the lawman tried to mutter something but a spray of blood blew from his lips and his eyelids fluttered closed.

Ruby was suddenly at his side, trying to hold him, trying to say something. He looked up at the madman standing in the street, seeing the vicious satisfaction of death filling the man-killer's black eyes.

'You sonofabitch!' Jim felt the urge to draw, even from his awkward position, surge over him. Stroud saw it, too.

'It ain't time, boy. You know it. I won't draw. And I know you ain't got it in you to kill me in cold blood.'

Ruby grabbed Jim's arm, trying to hold it, desperation and frantic worry in her eyes.

Cold fury rushing through him, he wanted to kill Stroud in that instant, see the shootist's lifeblood run out into the mud. But he was not a killer.

He held the mankiller's gaze, lips tight. 'You'll hang for this, Stroud. By hell I'll see to it.'

Stroud gave another laugh and tucked the star into a pocket. 'I'll never hang, boy. You know it well as I do. You got business with me I'll be in the saloon. Otherwise, stay out of my way.' Stroud walked off slowly and Jim let Ruby take him in her arms. Rain beat down on them, but he paid it no mind. It would take a hell of a lot more than rain to wash away the agony and loss he felt now.

★ ★ ★

For the second time that day Jim found himself at the cemetery. The cold rain beat down on him, running in streams off his Stetson, soaking his clothing. This time *he* was burying kinfolk, saying goodbye. He had carried his uncle here and dug the grave, muscles aching and heart leaden with sorrow. He stared down into the blackness of the gaping hole, feeling what Ruby had suffered earlier, the throbbing grief, the overwhelming sense of loss.

He swallowed against the emotion choking his throat, fought to hold back tears. His uncle was gone. A hell of a man senselessly gunned down by a killer with no sense of right or wrong, nothing resembling human compassion or mercy. Perhaps Stroud would claim self-defence. Perhaps not. It made little difference because now there was no law in Holliday, no marshal to bring justice.

But there was Jim Sutter and he damn well didn't need to prove anything. His uncle never would have tried to shoot it out with Stroud unless forced. Stroud had executed him and that was all there was to it.

Jim should have seen it coming. His uncle had issued a challenge to Stroud in the saloon the night before and the shootist would never let it go unanswered. But he hadn't expected a move like this so soon. Again he had made a mistake. And again Stroud had taken clean advantage of it.

Ruby stood to the side, face drawn, a lost look in her hazel eyes. She had witnessed premature death, understood what he felt. It strengthened the bond between them, brought them closer. She hadn't spoken, had simply helped him dig.

He shovelled dirt into the grave. Tomorrow he would see the funeral man about a marker and pay for the pine box he had taken from outside the cabinet shop.

Stroud.

The name burned in his mind; hate surged through his veins. The mankiller had raised the stakes. Stroud had judged him right: Jim would not shoot him down in cold blood, no matter how much he wanted to. But he would kill the shootist in a fair fight, or die trying. He had spent countless nights without sleep and countless others suffering with the nightmare of killing that other man, but he reckoned he would lose none over Stroud when the time came. He felt some sort of difference in him, now, a numb sense of duty and hunger for justice that overrode all compunction where killing a man like Stroud was concerned.

He would corner Stroud and force him into drawing.

Face set in dark lines, he threw the shovel aside and walked from the boneyard to his horse. He jammed a boot into the stirrup and mounted.

'Jim, please . . . ' Ruby said, halting at the gate. 'Please just take me home and we'll wait out the pain together. I know how it feels, I know how it eats your insides out.'

He gazed at her, swallowing hard, trying to keep back the swell of emotion and his resolve focused. 'I can't, Ruby. I got no choice.'

'He aims to kill you, Jim. That's plain to see. I'll let him have the land, we'll go away together. Please, I can't lose anyone else . . . '

Emotion clutched in his heart. He knew her feelings then, knew they matched his and accepted what he was, what he had done.

'I'm sorry . . . ' His words were a whisper, pregnant with regret. 'But if Stroud walks away nothing would ever be right — for either of us.'

He reined around, gigged his horse into a risky gallop; the bay's hooves slid and slapped in the muck of the rutted trail. He rode hard towards the saloon, where Stroud had said he would be, hands clutching the reins until his knuckles bleached bone-white.

He reached the saloon and dismounted, his body aching, yet driven by surges of hate and fury. His boots thudded like gunshots as he crossed the boardwalk.

He flung aside the batwings, stepped inside. His gaze scanned the bar, picking out Stroud, who was seated at a table, a whiskey in one hand, a book in the other.

As Jim took steps inward, cowhands and whores moved out of his way, wary of the icy look in his eyes.

Stroud looked up, mild surprise crossing his features. 'Hell, boy, you got here a lot quicker than I expected. You aim to kill me?' The man was mocking him and it increased the fury in his veins.

'Ain't no self-defence this time, Stroud. You killed in cold blood. I aim to see to it you don't do it again.'

Stroud tucked the book into his pocket. 'Get the hell out of here, boy.

I'll let you know when it's time to die.'

'It's time now, Stroud. For you.'

Stroud uttered a low laugh. 'You noble types are always the same, eager to get lead 'twixt their eyes and be done with it. I ain't that way, boy. For me killing takes time, needs savourin'. I'm still workin' on savourin' your uncle's.'

Rage overtook him and he lost all thought of coaxing Stroud into drawing. He flung himself at the gunslinger, who apparently hadn't expected the move.

Jim hit the shootist full force and sent him backwards over his chair, Jim coming down on top of him. The whiskey flew up as the table flew over, splashing the sawdust. A cloud of it billowed up as Stroud's back slammed into the floor.

Stroud tried to roll and Jim hurled a punch at the man's face, endeavouring to smash the gunslinger's nose into a bloody pulp.

Stroud jerked his head to the side

and Jim's knuckles struck the floor-boards with a resounding thud. Pain lanced through his hand and he cursed.

In that moment of distraction Stroud took full advantage. The killer twisted bringing a knee up into Jim's ribs. Agony shot through Jim's side and air exploded from his lungs.

Stroud was half up by the time Jim pushed himself to his hands and knees. He looked up to see Stroud's booted instep lashing towards his face.

He tried to roll with it, succeeded some, but the foot still smashed into his swollen lips and sent skewers of agony through his teeth. Blood filled his mouth with a gunmetal taste and he coughed a spray of crimson.

Reaching his feet, Stroud laughed. 'Hell, boy, you got more gumption than I reckoned.'

Jim wasted no time with words. He sprang to his feet and lunged, throwing a short punch as he drove forward. Stroud tried to sidestep, partially successful but Jim's blow grazed the gunslinger's temple. Stroud blinked and stepped back. Jim followed with an uppercut that caught the man squarely in the jaw. Stroud's eyes glazed an instant. He shook his head and muttered, 'Hell . . . '

Jim didn't wait for the gunslinger to get his bearings. He launched another blow towards the killer's face.

This time Stroud was ready for it, parried with a block and sent his own fist straight down the trail. Jim couldn't get his head out of the way; the blow hit him full force in the mouth. Stars exploded across his vision and his legs went out from under him.

He hit the floor, groaning, the room spinning. He struggled to get right back up but had little control over his muscles.

Stroud gave Jim no opportunity to gain his feet. The gunslinger grabbed two fistfuls of Jim's shirt and heaved him up. With a roar, the killer sent him hurling across a table. The table collapsed in a cloud of sawdust. Jim slammed into the floor on a shoulder and blackness rolled in like thunderclouds from the corners of his mind.

He lay there, barely conscious, breath beating out in hot gasps, pain wracking every conceivable area of his body. Hands grabbed him again and hauled him up, threw him into a chair. Vision blurry, he saw Stroud's face hovering above him.

Stroud laughed. 'You still ain't afeared of me, are ya, boy? It just ain't in your eyes. But the question's still there — you got what it takes to go on with this business? That's it, ain't it? You were lookin' to quit, couldn't make the decision? I'll be the answer, boy, but not while I'm celebratin'. You can count on it. Trouble is, once you get your answer it won't do you a lick of good. I'm gonna kill ya, boy. But I'll do it under my rules and my time of choosin'.' He grabbed Jim again and hurled him sideways. Jim hit the bottom of the bar and lay there, barely aware.

'Get the hell away from him, you

bastard!' A voice cut through his haze. He struggled to focus. Ruby had come through the batwings. Dripping wet, she ran towards Jim, dropped to his side and cradled his head.

Stroud tipped a finger to the brim of his hat, which he had found on the floor and put on. 'Ma'am, I'll be seein' you in a few days. You best think about leavin'.'

'You go to hell!' The words came with as much spite as she could muster.

'Eventually, I reckon . . . ' Stroud walked from the saloon and a heavy silence fell over the bar-room.

Jim's senses were returning, courtesy of the throbbing pain administered by Stroud.

'You're lucky he didn't kill you,' Ruby said and he supposed she had a right to scold, but her censure held little heart, mostly relief more than anything else.

She helped him to his feet and he took shaky steps. He let Ruby guide him outside to his horse and help him into the saddle. The fight had gone out of him and there was only pain, defeat, and a woman he wanted to cling to until the dawn washed away the demons of the night.

8

Jim drew up at the back of the house and dismounted. He'd been out surveying the grounds for any sign of Stroud, but had come up empty. In the five days since his uncle's death all had been deceptively tranquil. He had spent most of the time brooding, letting his mind wander over the past good times with his uncle, the happy times, the times Frank taught him to shoot and track and be a man. He had said goodbye in the only way he knew how, but that would never be enough to quell the sense of loss death lays on a man's soul.

Through it all only one thing brought any comfort. He had spent many hours talking with Ruby, growing closer to her than he had thought possible. Still even that was overshadowed by the threat approaching with this day.

The five days had passed with no

word from Stark or Stroud. Although Jim had made numerous excursions into Holliday in search of him, the mankiller seemed to have disappeared off the face of the earth. No one had seen him since that night at the saloon. He had kept watch on Stark's compound as well, but had spotted no sign of the shootist.

Maybe Stroud wouldn't come . . .

He would come all right. He was just using the wait to his advantage, making them wonder, get antsy. He was a master player and the technique was one Jim had used himself more than a few times manhunting. It caused men to make mistakes, got them rattled.

A sound.

In the distance, an ominous drumming of hoofbeats.

It's time . . .

A prickle of dread went through him. The hoofbeats came at a steady pace from the south, growing louder. He took a deep breath and eased around the corner.

Jim saw him then, riding in, tall in the saddle like some dark god riding from hell. A darkness seemed to ride in with him, a chilling wind. His duty plain, the mankiller's features were passive. He had come to enforce Stark's ultimatum and Ruby Pendelton would leave this land. Dead or alive.

The front door burst open and Jim saw her step out onto the porch, Winchester jammed to one shoulder, her finger bone-white on the trigger. He hadn't expected that; he had told her to stay in the house, grab the rifle and shoot first only if the mankiller tried to enter before Jim spotted him. He cursed, knowing it might annoy Stroud and cause him to shoot her before asking questions.

Jim remained still, not wanting to come around the house suddenly and force the gunfighter's hand prematurely. He eased his Peacemaker from its holster.

Stroud drew up, black eyes surveying the situation. A thin smile played on his lips. The gunslinger was likely well aware of Jim's presence there, just beyond the corner of the house; seasoned manhunters acquired the ability to sense things like that, and Stroud was as seasoned as they came.

Stroud's smile turned sardonic. 'You aim to kill me, ma'am? Or leave that to Sutter?'

Ruby's face darkened; hate shown in her eyes. 'Get off my land, Stroud, 'fore I pull this trigger and send you straight to hell.' Her voice didn't waver.

'Beg to differ, ma'am, but this here land will belong to Mr Stark shortly.' He slowly reached into a pocket of his duster and pulled out a rolled piece of paper tied with a red ribbon. He tossed it to the ground. 'Mr Stark's made you a right generous offer. You best sign it now, if'n you know what's good for you.'

Ruby dropped the Winchester's aim and pulled the trigger, blowing the rolled piece of paper to shreds, then lifting the rifle back to aim at Stroud.

'Get out of here.' Her tone came icy.

Stroud gazed at the remnants of the document and laughed. 'Doesn't matter a lick to me, ma'am. I'm here to take you off this land one way or the other.'

'You best leave, Mr Stroud, 'fore I pull this trigger again. Next time it won't be your worthless paper that gets blown to high hell.'

Stroud studied her, as if deciding whether she was serious and apparently concluding she was, because his face darkened. Jim wasn't sure then whether Stroud would draw on her. He gave the gunslinger a pretty good chance of getting his gun out and up and killing Ruby before she could get off a shot, based on what he had seen the other night.

Jim stepped from around the corner of the building and aimed his Peace-maker at Stroud. The shootist gazed at him and the mocking smile came back to his face. 'Sutter, still no fear, I see. No horse sense, neither.'

'You best do what the lady told you,

216

Stroud. You might get one of us but you won't get both.' Jim sighted the man's chest down his barrel.

Stroud took a deep breath. His saddle creaked as he shifted slightly, gaze flowing from Jim to Ruby, then back to Jim. Jim saw a measure of respect in the killer's eyes; Stroud knew the younger man held no fear and that was, at least for this moment, the equalizer.

Stroud gripped the reins. 'Not time yet, Mr Sutter. But will be soon.' He reined around and rode away and Jim said a silent thanks that Ruby hadn't been hurt.

When Stroud at last disappeared, Ruby lowered her rifle and started to tremble. He holstered his gun and went to her, putting an arm around her shoulders, guiding her into the house. He took the rifle and set it back on the wall rack.

'We haven't won, have we?' She looked at him with a plea in her eyes.

He shook his head. 'No. He'll be

back if we don't do something and next time it won't go so smooth. We just bought ourselves a little time, nothing more.'

She nodded, frowning. 'How long you reckon?'

'Not long. Day, two, maybe another. That's an outside estimate. Stark won't be happy 'bout this when Stroud reports back to him. He'll want this land even more 'cause you said no, like your father. But I reckon it will be up to Stroud, no matter what Stark wants. Stark can't control him and if he's got any sense at all he knows as much.'

She looked at the floor and her shoulders sank. 'Maybe we should give it up. We can go somewhere like you said — '

'That ain't an option, Ruby.' He took her shoulders in his hands and she looked into his eyes. 'Stark would have Stroud track us down for what's happened and Stroud would do it on his own just for the pleasure of it. Stark might not like hearin' no but Stroud likes hearin' it even less.'

Defeat washed across her features. 'Then we wait and fight it out and Stark takes this land, this house, everything my father and I built.'

Jim went to the window, gazing out. He saw little choice, fight and die now or run and die later, when Stroud tracked them down.

The only option left was making the first move, striking first and fast. Maybe that would give them some small advantage.

He turned and looked at Ruby. 'I'm riding out to Stark's compound when it's nightfall. I'll find your title and hope I can find somethin' on him that's worth a noose. It's the only thing I can think to do.'

A look of horror touched her eyes. 'It's too dangerous. If you're caught — '

His tone came harsher than he wanted it to, but frustration was eating at him. 'If I'm caught, what? He'll kill me? He's going to do that anyway, Ruby. This way maybe I can get enough to hang the man on with the help of a county marshal.'

'That still leaves Stroud.' Her voice faded.

'Yes, it does, and he won't be so easy to do somethin' about, but maybe he'll lay low if Stark goes down, for fear of being charged and hanged himself.'

Her tone sharpened and he knew she would have none of his cowflop. 'You don't believe that. He'll be there and he'll walk away after he kills you, way he has from every other killin'.'

Jim turned back to the window. She was right. He saw no use arguing it with her. He also saw little option. They were at a sore disadvantage and anything that hinted at evening those odds had to be tried. Maybe he just needed to do it. In all his career he had never once sat back and waited for some hardcase to come to him. He had made the moves, placed the bets.

He felt her hand slide around his waist and her head at his shoulder. She knew she couldn't change his mind and wouldn't try. Together, they stood waiting for the day to darken to night.

* * *

The Stark ranch compound lay still under the frosty moonlight. Outbuildings, splashed with alabaster light, appeared like demonic sentinels in the distance, guarding the devil's homestead. The night was crystal clear and cold as a witch's tit. Jim's breath came out in clouds.

He eased his horse closer, scanning the outbuildings and corrals for any signs of life, seeing none. At this late hour, the bunkhouse was dark, lights having been extinguished nearly an hour ago. Jim had been poised at the compound's edge for the better part of three hours. Watching, waiting, anticipating. Everything had to be done with skill and precision this time. He could not afford any mistakes if he wanted to live long enough to help Ruby out of her predicament.

And bring Stroud and the rancher to justice.

Stark had to have something incriminating in his possession — Ruby's title, forged deeds, lists of men on his payroll. A man like that was too good at covering his tracks not to have gathered up potential problems and locked them away. He would entrust no one else with that information. Jim figured the best bet was in that oversized safe in his parlour.

Guiding his horse closer, Jim reined up and dismounted. After tethering Ruthie to a tree branch he crept towards the main house. Its adobe walls nearly glowed, white-washed with moonlight.

Was Stroud nearby? That puzzled him and he found it impossible to predict. The manhunter had vanished for nearly a week before riding into the ranch today. What would he do now? He wondered how Stark would have taken the news of failure but bet he had held his tongue all the same, if he knew what was good for him.

He wondered how Stroud had taken it. Likely with vile bitterness and thoughts of getting even. It was a waiting game again, though likely not a long one. Stroud would let them simmer in the knowledge he would be returning to kill them, grow sloppy with anxiety, maybe let their guard down just a fraction; then he would strike. If there were a manhunter's Bible he bet Vinton Stroud knew every verse by heart and practised its gospel.

Half-crouched, he drew closer to the house, alert for any signs of life within, but the rooms were dark. He reached a side window he judged belonged to the parlour and raised it. A prickle of nerves took him and he hesitated. Something about it struck him as too easy. Like the day he had first ridden here, knowing though all seemed serene Stark had kept careful watch on him. The rancher had utter confidence in Stroud then, but after today's failure, did he still?

Maybe Stroud was close by, waiting in the darkness.

Or maybe Stark simply didn't worry about any open opposition. Who would be brash — or foolish — enough to come into his territory with the likes of Stroud on his side?

He eased inside. Shadows of furniture were outlined in the moonglow bleeding through the windows. Silence. Everything was deathly still. He waited, not moving until he discerned whether his entry had been overheard. Nothing, not a sound from any quarter. He should have been relieved, but wasn't. Something felt wrong, some sense inside tingling, telling him to watch his step.

He eased towards the huge safe and knelt beside it, drawing a slow breath to make himself relax. His fingers found the dial and he pressed his ear against the heavy metal door. He'd opened safes before, though he reckoned never one this modern. He was prepared for it to give him trouble and tried to focus all his concentration on listening for the thin sounds that indicated the tumblers were clicking off the combination. It was a delicate art, sometimes futile, nearly always frustrating, and he missed the number the first time around. The loudening rhythm of his heartbeat began to compete with the sound of the dial turning. He knew every second more he spent in the house trying to get this door open was another second closer to being discovered.

The point suddenly became moot.

Something crashed into the back of his head and the sound of the tumblers was lost in the roar cascading through his mind. Stars burst across his vision.

The *shick* of a struck lucifer sounded and a light flared; a man, arm out-stretched, holding a lantern.

He slumped to the floor, strength deserting him.

'Well, looks like I'm one up on Mr Stroud, doesn't it, boys?' said Rutherford Stark, holding the lantern in front of Jim and grinning like a fat mountain lion.

Jim's head spun as he tried to focus. Three men, besides Stark, two with Smith & Wessons, one with a Winchester, hovered close by. Jim knew one of them had pistol-whipped him. Another mistake. He'd been so intent on divining the combination he hadn't heard them sneak up on him. He might have suspected Stroud would guess he might come here to gather evidence on Stark, but he never expected the cattleman to anticipate it and arrange a welcoming committee.

Two of the men grabbed his arms and hauled him to his feet.

'You should have accepted my offer, Mr Sutter.' Stark leaned in, face smug. 'I don't like being said no to.'

The third man hit him in the stomach with a Winchester butt. Air exploded from his lungs and nausea rose in his belly.

'Lock him in the ice-house until Stroud shows up,' Stark said. 'Then we

226

can have him take that woman off that land and kill them both.'

The next moment the lights went out, as the man holding the Winchester struck him full across the face with the rifle butt.

9

Ruby Pendelton had spent all night by the window, waiting for Jim Sutter to return. Her fingers were twisted into white knots and dread had gripped her heart. He was late, too late. He should have been back hours ago, and as each moment dragged by she had grown more and more terrified something had happened to him.

She had told him it was too dangerous breaking into Stark's ranch. Why hadn't they just left? She knew Jim was right, that Stark and Stroud would try to hunt them down, but there was a chance they might vanish into the West, live some sort of normal life. At least it would have given them more time together; right now that's what mattered most to her. Some things were more important than land, or standing your ground against the likes of Stark or Stroud. Some things were more important than even justice.

A week ago she wouldn't have thought so. Had anyone bothered to ask she would have told them keeping what was rightfully hers and avenging her father's death meant everything. But now . . . now things were different. Now she had a spark of hope, a chance that her future wasn't filled with loneliness and sorrows of the past.

She was surely in love with Jim Sutter and she knew he was in love with her. Hell of a thing to have happen.

Especially in light of the fact that he was most likely . . .

Dead?

She shuddered, not wanting to think of the possibility, but unable to keep the notion corralled.

A numbed feeling of hopelessness took over. He should have been back by now. No two ways about it. Had he found something to hang Stark on he would have come back for her first, before riding for the county marshal.

He would have never left her here at the mercy of Stroud had he not planned on returning shortly.

Something had gone wrong. Terribly wrong.

What? Stroud. Had the renegade manhunter caught him? Killed him?

A rush of emotion surged over her being and chased the numbness away. She struggled to hold back tears and keep her thoughts clear. It wouldn't help to fall apart right now.

She had to do something. She couldn't wait here any longer. She had to cling to some small desperate hope he was still alive and needed her.

Her gaze settled on the Winchester resting on the wall pegs. It was still loaded and every bullet had Stroud's name on it if he had taken Jim from her.

She had taken Jim to task for being nothing better than a killer, having no more loftier purpose than simply putting lead into another body, the way Stroud did. But what she wanted to do now, *would* do now, was certainly far less noble than what Jim aspired to. Hers was little less base than white-hot vengeance.

She felt tears well and struggled to keep them from flowing. They would do no good. Only killing Stroud would help.

This time he wouldn't walk away from his punishment.

★   ★   ★

After informing Stark of his failure yesterday at the Pendelton place, Vinton Stroud had spent the previous night at Usher and most of the morning in the saloon. It galled him that a lowly woman and starry-eyed manhunter had gotten the better of him, forcing him to ride off empty-handed. Stark hadn't said much — and lucky for the bastard he hadn't or he would have ended up with the bullet intended for Ruby Pendelton — but Stroud had seen the condemnation in his cousin's eyes. A

231

coward had questioned his skill, his ability, and he wouldn't abide by that. But he would deal with Stark after disposing of Pendelton and Sutter. Stark, kin or no, would be just another grave in the New Mex landscape.

He gulped a slug of his whiskey; the liquor burned its way down his gullet. He poured himself another, thudding the half-empty bottle down on the table.

Irritation crawled through him like fire ants. No one got the better of Vinton Stroud. No one.

A sudden stabbing pain pierced his temple and his eyelids fluttered. Sweat broke out on his forehead and for an instant the bar-room blurred.

Tap-tap-tapping . . .

'Stroud . . . ' A voice from the front of the saloon brought him from his spell and he cursed himself for making another mistake, wallowing in his thoughts and letting the ghosts get close. He didn't like being surprised. Sutter had surprised him with his move a few nights ago. Stroud never expected the boy to just lunge at him. Draw, maybe, but that had been a minor error and he had corrected it easily enough.

Then yesterday's fiasco at the Pendelton place. He reckoned that was not totally his fault. Stark had tied his hands, insisting he present Ruby Pendelton with the option of signing that paper.

But this, now this was something totally unexpected. He'd been caught flat-footed, a-swim in his own annoyance with events.

He slowly lifted his gaze towards the batwings. Ruby Pendelton stood just inside the saloon, her gaze locked to him. In bleached hands, she clenched a Winchester, its butt jammed to her shoulder, its barrel casting him a deadly one-eyed stare. She remained silent, but the look of hate on her face said everything. She had come to kill him.

Hell, he couldn't rightly believe it. He had never considered the likelihood of her coming after him, at least not without Sutter, and not with the look that was in her eyes. But lo and behold there she was, aiming that goddamn thing at him with the full intent of pullin' the trigger.

But why? What gave her the gumption? Surely not just the prospect of losing her land, or the fact he had killed her father. Had that been the case she would have done this a week ago. No, something had happened he didn't know about, hadn't anticipated. He let out a disgusted breath. Whatever it was it was another miscalculation on his part and they were starting to pile up.

She stood, gaze locked with his for long moments and he waited until she was ready to make the first move. He might be able to get his gun out in time, but from the awkward sitting position and her finger caressing the Winchester's trigger he debated the sense in that option. The Winchester might go off anyway. Even dead men twitched. No, better she opened the play.

Eyes narrowing, she took slow measured steps across the bar-room and stopped a half-dozen feet from him, eyes never shifting, aim never wavering. While he saw she plainly intended to kill him, he sensed something else . . . what was it?

Something she needed to know. That was it. A question. He relaxed just a hair, knowing that bought him time.

'What you waitin' on, ma'am?' His voice was steady, low.

'Outside, Mr Stroud . . . '

He didn't think he'd ever heard more ice in a voice, even his own and he was a goddamn expert at it. 'Ma'am, you're makin' the last mistake of your life . . . '

'Am I? Don't see it that way, Mr Stroud. I see it as you're gonna tell me what happened to Jim and then you're goin' to your final for what you done.'

So that was it. Something had happened to Sutter.

'Reckon I don't catch your meanin'. I ain't seen Sutter since yesterday.'

'I don't believe you. What have you

done with him?'

He studied her: she didn't shake, didn't waver. Hell, he had seen less brave men and he almost admired her for that.

'I ain't seen him, ma'am. That's the God's honest truth.'

'Reckon you wouldn't know what that was if'n it bit you in the britches, Mr Stroud.'

'Now, why don't you just sit yourself on down and we'll talk it over nice and friendly like — '

'Get outside!' Ruby shouted, anger flashing in her eyes.

He slowly stood and she backed away a few feet, never once taking her sights off him. He held up his hands, palms outward and edged towards the batwings, stopping. She motioned with the Winchester and he walked outside into the morning sunlight. He suddenly felt the rifle barrel digging into his back and a thin smile took his lips. Good. That was better. An amateurish mistake.

'What's happened to Sutter, ma'am? I'm tellin' you straight I got no notion why you're aimin' to kill me. Even a condemned man gets read the charges.'

'He went to Stark's last night to get evidence against him and you know it.'

Ah, so that was it. Sutter had moved against Stark and the cattleman had somehow found a temporary horseshoe and captured — *killed* him? Bastard. Things were really stacking up on the sundown side, weren't they?

A stab of pain took him again, knifing into his temples. His eyelids fluttered and sweat broke out across his forehead.

No. Not now, not . . .

Deep into that darkness peering . . .

Now.

The pain subsided. He let out a breath.

'An' he ain't come back, that it?' he asked.

'You know it well as I do.'

' 'Fraid I don't. You see if I had Sutter he'd be dead and you'd be dead. I wouldn't be standin' here discussin' it with you.'

He moved, a blur of motion, as he whirled, and brought an arm up, contacting the Winchester's barrel and deflecting it sideways. She jerked the trigger. A deafening blast sounded and he swore he felt lead skim by his cheek in a sizzling kiss and that was just too goddamn close. He saw the startled look on her face but that quickly vanished, as he brought his fist up in a blow that sent her backwards into the wall and the Winchester skittering down the boardwalk.

★　★　★

Throbbing pain in her face brought Ruby back to consciousness. Confusion took her and she struggled to gain control of her senses. The agony in her teeth and chin increased as she grew more aware, and she wondered if the bastard had broken her jaw.

Opening her eyes, she tried to focus. Her body ached from the cramped position she was in on the floor, her arms stretched over her head, wrists lashed to a set of bars across a window.

Where was she?

The last thing she recollected was being outside the saloon with Stroud, ready to blow him to Kingdom Come. Now she was here, wherever here was.

Her gaze swept along a room roughly twenty by fifteen feet, stopping at a collection of objects piled high in a corner. She stared at them, wondering, then spotted something near the bottom, a gold watch on a chain she recognized as belonging to her father, the one Stroud had taken when he killed him. Beside the watch was the little doll her mother had made her; it had been in her pocket when she went to confront Stroud. A chill went through her. Stroud was even more of a monster than she thought, acquiring trophies from his kills as if those lives lost were nothing more than perverted sport.

Moving on, her attention travelled to the table holding a lantern and to the walls riddled with bullet holes, to the shattered black fragments of some sort of statue on the floor.

Attracted by a scraping noise, her gaze stopped abruptly, lifted. A gasp escaped her lips and her heart stuttered.

Stroud stood peering at her through a hole in a wall of brick. A wall that used to be an open doorway. He placed another brick into the shrinking aperture, fitting it precisely. She heard the scrape of his trowel smoothing out dung mortar. He was bricking her up in this room, wherever it was, imprisoning her for all eternity. Horror went through her. She pulled at the ropes lashing her wrists to the bars, but they wouldn't loosen. They cut into her flesh, grew slick with blood.

'I was tellin' the truth, ma'am.' Stroud's voice came steady, purposeful. 'I didn't know where Sutter was, but I will and he'll join you. But his death will be a hell of a lot faster than yours. You see, I can't abide miscalculations and obstinance, and you caused me some. I want to make sure you got plenty of time to think it over. Don't you worry none, though, you got plenty of company in these walls. You ain't the first guest who ain't left Usher.'

Her lips moved but no sound came out. Stroud was plumb loco and she would die here, slowly starving and thirsting and stinking in her own urine. No one would ever know.

Stroud grinned. An insane light danced in his black eyes. ' 'The thousand injuries of Fortunato I had borne as best I could; but when he ventured upon insult, I vowed revenge.' Ain't a poem verse, ma'am, but I reckon it's appropriate . . . '

He laughed and slid the last brick into place.

★ ★ ★

Vinton Stroud was right proud of himself. He'd turned a mistake into an advantage and dealt appropriately with the Pendelton woman. Soon he would have Sutter as well if Stark hadn't killed him, which he doubted the cattleman had the balls to do on his own. There was a room and plenty of bricks left over for Stark if he had by some chance.

Approaching the Bar S compound, he drew up, spotting one of Stark's 'hands guiding a horse into the stable. He recognized the animal: Sutter's bay. He smiled and sent his horse towards the ranch house.

Reaching the house, he dismounted and stepped across the veranda. Entering, he located Stark in the parlour. A burst of anger swept over the cattleman's eyes as he turned.

Stroud glared and the man shrank back, eyes darting. 'You best watch your look, Stark. I ain't in the best of attitudes.'

Stark visibly shuddered. 'Where you been?'

'My business ain't none of your concern. Where's Sutter?'

Surprise crossed the cattleman's face. 'How'd you know I had him?'

'Had me a nice parley with Ruby Pendelton. She was right worried about him. Where is he? You best not have killed him.'

Stark shifted feet. 'He's locked in the icehouse.'

'Alive?'

Stark nodded. 'Hell, yes. I want you to kill him then go take that Pendelton woman off that land and bury her.'

Stroud came deeper into the room. 'She's no longer a problem.'

'Hell you say?'

Stroud drilled him a look that made the cattleman clamp his mouth shut.

'You got any dynamite 'round this hole?'

Stark nodded. 'There's some in the supply shack. What the hell you want dynamite for?'

Stroud ignored the question. He felt no need to explain his reasoning to a dead man. 'Call your men together and tell them to ride out for the day.'

Stark's face went red. Spittle flecked the corners of his mouth. 'Have you lost your goddamn mind?'

A look crossed Stroud's face and he felt a surge of anger at the cowardly powermonger who was his kin. Stark realized the outburst was a mistake and took a backwards step.

'You go with them. Don't come back till sundown. Where's Sutter's gun?'

Stark nodded towards the safe.

'Open it.' Stroud nudged his head towards it. Stark complied and removed the gunbelt and Peacemaker, passed it to Stroud after closing the door.

'I hope you got a notion what you're

doin',' Stark didn't say it any too confidently.

'I hope you got a notion who you're talkin' to.'

An hour later, Stroud stood alone, staring out at the empty spread. Stark and his men had ridden off for town and when they got back at dusk Stroud would be finished and back to deal with the cattleman.

He went into the house and got Sutter's gunbelt and Peacemaker, first emptying the chamber of bullets, then holstering it. Going to the ice-house, he tossed the belt a few feet from the door, then pulled the Poe book from his pocket and pitched it to the ground beside the rig.

Moments later, he came from the supply shed with a stick of dynamite and twenty feet of fuse. He jammed the dynamite between the lock and door, ran the fuse outwards, making sure it was straight.

* * *

Jim Sutter awoke chilled, face aching. Darkness came with the cold and he remained still for long moments. He felt of his jaw; it was swollen and pained like a sonofabitch, but that was probably the least of his problems.

He struggled to his feet, muscles stiffer than it seemed they should have been, but he reckoned the cold had something to do with it.

Where was he? Arms outstretched, he felt around in the darkness. He recognized the scent of hay and dirt and sawdust. The chill bit into him, made his bones ache. He encountered a smooth cold slab of something and it took him a moment to figure out what he had touched, then it came to him: ice. Blocks of it packed with sawdust. By feel, he made his way around the interior, tripping into the cakes of ice numerous times, banging his shins and cursing. He discovered he was imprisoned in a small square room with thick insulating walls and no windows. Stark had put him in the ice-house. He reckoned he was lucky the man hadn't just shot him, but he figured the coward would leave that pleasure to Stroud.

He located the door and gave it a shove. Locked, likely with a heavy padlock of some sort on the outside. He threw himself against it; the door shuddered, but didn't budge. Contemplating the grim situation, Jim wondered how much time he had before Stroud showed up to finish him off. But thoughts of his own predicament came second to the knowledge that with him trapped in here, Ruby was alone and easy prey for the mankiller.

With a burst of panic he threw himself against the door over and over, bellowing shouts and curses until his shoulder and arm went numb and he could barely stand. He fell to his knees, gasping.

Hours passed, time dragging, thoughts torturing him. He had always courted death in a way; it was a risk every manhunter faced and he had never really given it much thought. Until now. He felt no fear of it for himself; he was afraid for Ruby. With her he had found something, a direction, a focus in life that meant he had looked at the two trails and finally known which one to take. But that wouldn't matter if he couldn't save her.

A short time later, light trickled in. Dawn. The sun had risen. Before long a dull glow turned into streamers of light that bled along the crack between the door and frame.

He considered pounding on the door again but decided it would do no good. Men moved about outside, but they worked for Stark and none would lift a hand against the cattleman.

The coldness was getting to him. His body felt stiffer and he was starting to stumble. He wrapped his arms around himself and moved around with more vigour, but it helped little.

Hours passed and no further sound came from the outside. That struck him as odd. It was nearing the height of the day, he judged, and surely the compound would be a beehive of activity. But he heard nothing, as if the men had deserted the ranch.

'You best move far back from the door, Mr Sutter,' a voice called out and a deeper chill went through him.

'Stroud?'

'I'll be using dynamite on it in a few moments and I would prefer you didn't die that way.'

Jim moved back, wondering what the man was up to. 'What the hell you doin', Stroud?'

'I'm gonna kill you, Mr Sutter. Oh, but not this way, don't you worry. I'm going to savour it. I'll be waitin' for you, along with the filly you got a hankerin' for.'

Jim's belly plunged. 'You have Ruby?'

'I got her. Course, she won't last much longer, I reckon.'

'Don't hurt her, Stroud. I'll give you whatever you want.'

'I reckon you will, Mr Sutter. Your gun's here outside. I expect you'll provide me with more opposition than your uncle?' Stroud laughed.

Anger boiled in Jim's veins. 'Where will I find you, Stroud?'

' 'Over the mountains,' Mr Sutter, 'down the Valley of the Shadow . . . ' '

Jim's brow knotted. 'What the hell does that mean?'

'You'll figure it out.'

He heard the jangle of Stroud's spurs recede as the mankiller walked away. A few seconds later, the sound of hoofbeats galloped into the distance. He waited what seemed like endless moments, crouched in the far corner of the ice-house, blocks of sawdust-covered ice between him and the door.

An explosion shattered the stillness and the concussion battered him like he'd been thrown from a bronc and landed on hardpack. Ears ringing, he staggered to his feet, fighting the blackness that crowded in from the corners of his mind, and out into the swirling clouds of dust and sunlight. The warmth of the day contrasted starkly with the chill of the ice-house. As his body thawed, he jumped about, struggling to get the circulation back into his chilled limbs and regain his equilibrium.

Spotting his rig lying in the dust a few feet away, he went to it. He gathered it up and strapped it around his waist. A book lay beside the belt. He stared at it a moment, then he picked it up. A collection of poetry by Poe. Why had the mankiller left that?

It took him a little over fifteen minutes to find the line Stroud had spoken, in a poem called 'Eldorado'.

Eldorado . . .

Something came to him. The area was littered with mining towns gone bust. The largest ghost town was called Eldorado, he recollected, and that was a good four miles from here. Was that where Stroud had vanished to after murdering Jim's uncle?

It had to be. No one would think of looking in a ghost town for him.

Jim pocketed the book and went

towards the stable, his steps getting steadier.

He found his horse and saddle and moments later climbed onto the mount.

Eldorado. Stroud awaited him there and it all came down to a moment in a man's life. A decision. Right or wrong. Life or death. His uncle had made it, to a wrong end. Now it was Jim's turn and he saw no choice at all. If there was a chance Ruby was alive and could be saved he had to take it.

He gigged his horse into a ground-eating gallop. The Devil awaited him in Eldorado.

10

'Christalmighty . . . ' Jim muttered, as he reined to a halt at the junction of Eldorado. He froze there in the saddle for long moments, gaze sweeping over the aggregation of adobe and plank, brick and log; the Gothic and Greek Revival styles; the sod and beam roofing. Early afternoon sunlight glinted from the windows and glazed the structure with an eerie glow. A sense of perverse awe filled him.

The mankiller awaited him in that house; Jim felt sure of it. Stroud had lured him here and the bait was Ruby, the price a confrontation of skills, one that would feed the shootist's bloodlust, his addiction to killing. The mankiller was likely even watching Jim's approach at this very minute.

Jim urged his bay forward, towards the thing of monstrous symmetry.

Hands tightening on the reins, he drew a steadying breath as another wave of dread washed over him. Had Stroud kept Ruby alive? He had indicated as such but Jim couldn't be sure. He mouthed a silent promise to a likely unhearing Maker that if he got them out of this he would choose a life with her and leave manhunting behind.

Drawing up, he dismounted, eyes roving and senses alert for any sign of movement, or threat.

He peered at the front door, which lay open, inviting, dark. Genies of dust whirled across the porch boards and wind sang eerie songs through the eaves.

He stepped across the porch, legs tense, heart beginning to pound with anxiety.

Entering, gaze scanning every direction, he discovered the anteroom empty. The mankiller was nowhere to be seen; he was somewhere deeper in the house.

The interior was just as randomly

patterned and laid out as the exterior and it didn't surprise him. Slipping his Peacemaker from its holster, he took cautious steps.

'Welcome to Usher, Mr Sutter . . . '

The voice came hollow and distant and startled the hell out of him. He stopped, peering about the empty room, gun swinging left then right, searching for any sign of the man who had uttered those words. He saw no one.

His gaze lifted, settled on a small metal tube embedded into the wall just above his head. A metal screening covered the end of the tube. That's where the mankiller's voice had come from. Stroud was speaking from some hidden location within the house.

He started forward, suppressing the urge to shiver. A click sounded.

A sudden shuddering sent Jim lunging sideways, bringing up his Peacemaker in the same move. His attention jerked to a silhouetted figure that had sprung up in front of him. He fired without thought, a simple smooth reflex.

The hammer fell with an empty click and he let out a curse.

'Your first mistake, Mr Sutter,' came the voice. 'I removed the bullets from your gun. Rest assured, though, I will give you one back when the time comes . . . *if* the time comes.' A laugh followed, echoing hollowly from the tube.

Jim holstered his Peacemaker, disgusted with himself for not checking whether his gun was loaded.

He gazed at the figure before him and frowned. It was merely a wooden cut-out in the shape of a man painted black. The click he had heard beforehand told him he'd likely stepped on some spot on the floor that activated a spring mechanism, sending the thing into his path.

He would have to be more careful. The next one might not be so harmless.

'Ruby?' he yelled, edging around the cut-out.

'Hell, she's here, Mr Sutter. Don't you worry none. You just got to find her. You might even be in time 'fore the mortar sets.'

Stroud was taunting him, trying to unnerve him, and doing a damn good job of it. What did he mean by mortar setting?

He moved forward along the zigzagging path the hall followed, coming to a parlour with antagonistic wall colours and paper.

His heart pounded faster and sweat trickled down his face. The house was getting to him, along with Stroud's taunting.

Another click caught his ear. He cursed. He had stepped on —

A shrieking swish sounded and Jim instinctively threw himself forward. The move saved his life, but just barely.

He hit the floor and rolled, coming back up in a crouch.

The swish had come from the descending blade of a huge pendulum. Stepping on another booby-trapped spot, he had activated a mechanism that released the great glittering crescent from a wall niche. The blade cleaved a path across the room, disappearing into a cavity in the opposite wall. Immediately coming back out, it swung back and forth in a deadly shivering arc with an explosive current of air that rattled daguerreotypes, paintings and lantern chimneys.

The blade jerked lower with each pass. Jim watched in morbid fascination, mesmerized by its gleaming motion. A moment later, razored steel cleaved into the floorboards with a shriek of rending wood. A heavy silence filled the room and Jim let out the breath he'd been holding. He'd been lucky. Had he reacted an instant slower the thing would have sliced him in two.

He straightened, struggling to get his heart out of his throat.

'Congratulations, Mr Sutter. You might just make it. Best watch your step from now on . . .'

'You're loco, Stroud, plumb loco!'

A laugh sounded, echoing from the walls and through Jim's soul.

Jim edged out of the room, studying each wall for any signs of an opening, each step for any concealed mechanism he might activate.

He moved down another diagonal hall, reaching a stairway without a rail. The staircase appeared to come right out of the wall and anyone wanting to go up would have to hop on from the side. The corridor stretching before him descended at a gentle slope beneath the upper floor. An iron tire chandelier hung from the ceiling six feet above the level of the top step. He peered up at a closed door at the top of the stairs.

Two trails?

Which one did he take? The wrong choice might lead to instant death.

What was it Stroud said? Watch his step? Maybe that was some sort of clue. The steps. Was Ruby behind that door somewhere? Or was it a trick to get him to go up there, to meet death?

'Where do you go next, Mr Sutter?'

259

the voice came again and he saw another of the speaker tubes in the stairway wall.

The steps might be a trap.

They might not.

He chose the hallway and eased forward, heart beating a step faster. A hundred feet farther, the hallway turned at a ninety-degree angle. When he rounded the corner, he discovered it ended in a brick wall.

A burst of realization took him and he spun, hurling back along the hallway. He had made the wrong choice; it had to be another trap.

A harsh grating sounded as the ceiling began to lower. A metal door was descending at the end of the hall where he had entered, its base a blade, razor-sharp.

'What is it like to be buried alive, Mr Sutter, crushed out of existence? I expected more from you. Don't disappoint me, boy.'

Jim barely heard Stroud's taunt. His heart was roaring in his ears and breath burned in his throat. He had mere seconds before the door closed, sealing off the exit, leaving him to be crushed.

The door dropped another foot. The space beneath was only about three feet high now. The ceiling had lowered a good two feet and was nearly touching his Stetson.

He dived, arms outstretched, hurtling forward with sheer momentum slamming into the floor on his chest. The door jerked down another foot. With mere inches to spare, he scrambled under the descending door. The blade-like bottom caught his foot before he cleared it completely, trapping him. With a vicious yank he came out of his boot.

The door fell closed, slicing the boot in two and he let out a ragged breath. Sweat poured down his face. His heart pounded in his throat and he sat there for long moments, drawing deep breaths, struggling to regain his composure.

'Should have tried the stairs, Mr

Sutter. I gave you that. Your second mistake, Mr Sutter. Don't make another.'

Jim pushed himself up, gaining unsteady legs. Swallowing hard, he peered at the stairs. Was Ruby up there? He had no choice but to take that chance. It was either go up or back the way he came.

He started up, heart hammering. Each step taken was a held breath, a gasped relief when nothing happened.

A few more.

Three. Two . . .

He reached the top step and set a foot down —

He felt the mechanism click, but it did little good. With a snapping shudder, the top three steps dropped out from beneath him. He couldn't throw himself backward and reach solid steps in time.

Falling, he reflexively pitched forward, making a wild grab for the glass doorknob, getting it. The jolt as he caught the handle nearly tore his arm from its socket. His hat tumbled into the nothingness beneath him. Pain spiked his shoulder as he strained to hold on. Fighting back the agony, he glanced down. 'Judas Priest!' he muttered.

Nearly twenty feet below was a floor of spikes. They jutted straight up, thick steel at least two feet long and placed close together. If he fell, he'd be skewered.

'Very good, Mr Sutter, but what next?'

His fingers, damp with sweat, were starting to slip. He could only maintain his hold a few seconds more. The pain in his shoulder was sending slivers of agony down his arms.

He kicked up, getting a boot on the three-inch lip of the doorway. He would have one chance at this. If he failed . . .

Bracing his foot against the frame, he struggled to turn the knob, praying it wasn't locked.

It wasn't. The door swung inward. Using his leg, he shoved against the frame and rolled over the threshold.

He lay there panting, heart thundering. His arm felt numb, but he forced himself to his feet. Another hall lined with doors stretched out before him. Was Ruby behind one of them? Was Stroud?

'Ruby!' he yelled, sweat streaming down his face.

'Jim!' Her voice came muffled, but close, and a wave of relief surged through him.

The feeling was short lived. An odour reached his nostrils: smoke, coming from somewhere below. Christamighty, had Stroud set the place on fire?

'Ruby where are you?' he called with renewed panic.

'I'm in a room. Stroud bricked up the door.'

Jim's gaze started along the hall, stopped. He spotted dust from dried mortar and scrapes from possibly a barrow on the floor next to the first door on his right.

He grabbed the handle, jerked open

the door. A brick wall blocked the entryway. He ran his fingers over the rough surface and joints. The mortar was damp but setting fast. He launched a kick at the wall, praying it hadn't set enough to become impenetrable.

The impact shuddered through his body. The area he had kicked bowed inward slightly but didn't give. He kicked at it again and again, harder each time, until a brick gave, flew inward, then another, creating a small opening. He kept kicking, until blood dampened the inside of his boot and agony radiated through his heel. He got the hole opened just big enough to accommodate his frame and clambered inside. He hobbled to her, foot numb from the repeated impact, swelling.

Untying her wrists from the bars, he lifted her into his arms, holding her tight and not wanting to let go. Tears ran down her face and she kissed him, sobbing.

He pulled back, held her shoulders, gaze locking with hers. 'Stroud set the place a-fire; we have to get out quick.'

She looked at him, eyes taking in the damage he had sustained, filling with worry. 'You're hurt . . . '

'I'll be all right from what's happened so far. Can't promise we'll get out of here in one piece, though. The place is filled with death traps.'

Limping, he took her elbow and guided her towards the opening in the bricks.

'Wait!' She went to the accumulation of objects and picked up a watch. 'My father's. Stroud took it when he killed him.' She tucked it in her pocket then grabbed a ragged little doll and shoved that into her skirt as well.

Jim climbed through the hole. Ruby followed and they went to the doorway leading to the lower level, stopping.

'Stairs dropped out,' he said. 'There's spikes below.' He glanced backward, frowning. 'There's no other way down. The hallway ends at a windowless wall. I reckon those other doors lead to brick walls or other rooms with barred windows and we don't have time to go lookin' through each one.' He glanced at the iron tire chandelier, swallowed hard.

'How do we get down?' Ruby asked.

He looked at her. 'We don't have a hell of a lot of choice. Grab hold of my back and don't let go.'

She nodded and climbed on and he drew a deep breath, gathering every ounce of strength he had left. His heart started to pound.

He leaped. For an instant he seemed suspended in the air, then falling forward in some slow motion death plunge. He let out a yell that snapped short as his fingers caught the chandelier's rim.

As his arms jerked straight, welts of excruciating pain sang through his shoulder. He hung there by his fingertips, Ruby clinging to his back.

He couldn't hold on. The weight on his back and pain in his shoulder were too much. His fingers pried loose and they plunged fourteen feet to the floor, landing hard, momentarily stunned.

Smoke clogged the lower hall. It billowed in from the parlour in thickening black clouds. Tongues of flame licked at the door frame. Loud crackling punctuated by snapping pops that sounded like shots reached his ears, as fire devoured papering and wood.

He got to his feet then helped Ruby up. She could barely stand. Her left ankle was twisted oddly, likely broken.

He put his arms beneath hers and guided her forward. They made their way through the parlour, using as much caution as possible not to step on any hidden mechanisms, but they had little time left.

Black smoke thickened into a dense pall, making it difficult to see, and choking his lungs. Ruby coughed violently, stumbled, barely able to walk, and he had to half drag her. His heel pained and he staggered, having trouble sustaining both their weights. Smoke stung his eyes and tears streaked dirty trails down his face. The heat became blistering, turning his face beet red, singeing his eyebrows. Flame leapt up the walls, dancing across the floor-boards.

They reached the ante-room and skirted the cut-out. 'I can't make it,' Ruby screamed, faltering. 'Go on without me!' She collapsed at his side. He gathered her in his arms and lifted, carrying her despite the pain and weakness gripping him. He would never leave without her. If she perished, he did too.

With a final burst of strength he lunged forward, going through the door, stumbling out into the cool October air and waning sunlight.

Reaching the middle of the street, he set her down and dropped to his knees, sucking in great gulps of fresh air. Sweat ran down his face in dirty streaks. Ruby, coughing, gasping, struggled to get up.

'Congratulations, Sutter. You've presented me with the challenge I was looking for. Now killin' you will be all the better.'

Through stinging eyes, Jim looked up to see the shootist standing there in the street, black duster fluttering in the breeze, pulled back so that the polished black metal of his Devil's Peacemaker glinted with sunlight.

Jim straightened, legs rubbery, and nudged his head towards the burning mansion. 'Why, Stroud?' he mouthed.

A dark grin spread across Stroud's lips. 'Even Usher had to fall, Mr Sutter. Today just seemed like the day.'

Jim saw the insanity in his eyes, then something else. Stroud's lips fluttered and his face washed blank, but only for an instant.

'You aim to kill me in cold blood now, Stroud? Ain't your style, is it?' He took a step towards the man, the demon in black.

Stroud's black eyes narrowed. 'You're right, Mr Sutter. It ain't my style.' Stroud eased his Peacemaker from its holster and rolled the chamber, letting four bullets drop into the dust and a fifth into his palm. He kept the sixth in the chamber. After slipping the gun back into the holster, he tossed the fifth bullet into the dust at Jim's feet. Jim knelt and picked it up, loading it into his own gun.

'One bullet each, Mr Sutter. Now you got a sportin' chance.'

The hell he did but it was better than nothing.

Gun in its holster again, Jim's hand hovered inches above the handle. Stroud's eyes met his, waiting, eager. Jim held his gaze.

' 'Deep into that darkness peering',' Stroud muttered and suddenly his eyelids fluttered again. Pain flashed across the mankiller's face. Jim glimpsed it and seized the split second of opportunity to make his draw.

Ruby screamed behind him, the sound drawn out and pleading, echoing through the dusty street.

Stroud let out a bellow, overcoming whatever spell had taken him. His hand swept to his gun.

But whatever had affected Stroud added a hair of a second to his draw time.

Jim pitched sideways as he drew, bringing his Peacemaker to aim in the same move. An untested skill.

The gunshots thundered at the same time, combining into one sound. Acrid blue clouds billowed from both Peacemakers.

Jim was still falling sideways. He expected to feel the searing agony of Stroud's bullet punching deep into his chest but that never came. Instead a welt of pain sizzled across his shoulder as lead opened a gory trench in his flesh.

Stroud stood frozen in the street. A blank look washed over his features.

Jim slammed into the ground and rolled. He came up on his elbows and back. His gaze locked on the mankiller.

Stroud crumpled, going down slowly, blood spurting from his mouth. He fell face-first into the dirt. A cloud of dust wafted up, settling in a fine film over him. Jim stared at the body then at the smoking Peacemaker in his hand, frozen inside. For only the second time in his career he'd been forced to kill a man. The feeling was one he'd never get used to.

He had known one of them would die, but that did little to ease the feeling. It could have just as easily have been him lying in the dust. Stroud might have seen Jim's move coming under other circumstances and likely beaten him. Perhaps Ruby's yell had distracted the shootist just enough, or perhaps whatever spell had gripped him had evened the odds.

Or perhaps the gunfighter had been simply too cocky and underestimated Jim's speed and skill. It didn't rightly matter. The threat of Vinton Stroud was ended and if ever a man had deserved death Stroud had.

Jim gained his feet and saw Ruby rushing towards him. He walked to Stroud, Ruby by his side, and peered down at the body of the man who had murdered her father and his uncle, the demon who had destroyed so many lives. He took the book from his pocket, the collection of poetry by Poe Stroud had left to guide him to Eldorado, and tossed it to the dirt.

' 'And, as his strength failed him at length . . . ' ' he whispered, face grim. ' 'He met a pilgrim shadow . . . '.'

Behind them, a huge section of the house collapsed with a great shrieking of wood and billowing of sparks and smoke. Flames roared up into the sky.

And Usher fell.

★ ★ ★

'What the goddamn hell?' Rutherford Stark mumbled, as he looked out of the parlour window. Jim watched the cattleman from behind, the rancher unaware he had snuck into the ranch house.

A week and a day had passed since Vinton Stroud fell and Jim knew by now Stark was likely antsy, wondering what had happened to his cousin. Jim would have come for Stark sooner, but had needed time to fetch the county marshal and his men, and the posse was likely what Stark was seeing ride in, now. Jim could hear the distant pounding of hooves and the shouts of the lawmen, as well as curses from Stark's 'hands. He had asked the marshal to grant him fifteen minutes to get into the house and give him time to find evidence against the cattleman.

Stark cursed and turned from the window, his corpulent features ruddy with panic. Every bit the coward, Stark was turning tail before the marshal's men raided the house.

Rutherford Stark froze as Jim's Peacemaker came up and levelled at his head. The heavy man's features bleached. His eyes darted and he ran a tongue over dry lips.

'How the hell did you get in here?' His voice shook.

Jim let an easy smile filter onto his

lips. 'Stroud sends his condolences from hell, Mr Stark.'

'He's . . . dead?' The cattleman's face went whiter and Jim felt a surge of satisfaction.

'Open the safe.' He motioned with the gun.

Stark started to quake and his mouth moved in silent protest. 'Look, Sutter, I'm a rich man. I can pay you more than you'd make in a lifetime and the offer to work for me still stands.'

Jim uttered a derisive laugh. 'Much as I'm tempted, Mr Stark . . . ' His voice dropped. 'Open the safe.'

Stark complied, hands shaking as he worked the dial.

The front door burst open and the marshal and two deputies came into the parlour, eyeing Jim.

Stark glanced at them, at Jim, back to the safe. He pulled open the door. Jim saw it lying there on the shelf, a derringer amongst the stacks of papers and boxes of valuables.

'Go ahead, Mr Stark. Go for the gun

if you think you can beat me.' Jim kept his eye dead on Stark, waiting for any sign the man had made the decision to fight his way out.

It didn't come.

Stark stepped back and Jim, keeping him covered, went to the safe. Shuffling through the stacks, he located Ruby's title, forged deeds and a number of other incriminating papers. The marshal took them, scanned the documents.

A confident expression came onto his face. 'There's enough to hang him on, Sutter, no doubt about that.'

Jim frowned. 'He'll walk if you bring him to trial, Marshal. He owns the lawyer in town and plenty of higher ups, I reckon.'

Stark looked suddenly frightened beyond his ability to control and started blubbering. 'You can't! I'm a rich man. I have power in these parts. I'm entitled to a fair trial.' That told Jim plain the rancher knew he could buy his way out of any sentence.

'It ain't legal and it ain't usual, but I'm plumb inclined not to see a man like this go free.' The marshal nodded to his deputies, who came over and took each of Stark's arms. They dragged him towards the door.

'No! You can't do this! It ain't legal. You can't — '

Jim looked at him. 'No, it ain't legal, Mr Stark. But neither was what you did to Ruby Pendelton when you hired Stroud to kill her pa. That makes you an accessory to murder.'

They hauled Stark outside. The marshal's men held some of the ranch-hands, the ones who hadn't pulled stakes and bolted for safe country. Jim saw the three who had helped Stark capture him a little over a week ago.

'Maybe we should hang them, too?' With a nudge of his head, the marshal indicated the men, who went white and started to protest.

Jim smiled. 'Way I figure it, if they see their way to testifying 'bout Mr Stark's activities and against the crooked lawyer they might take their chances with a fair trial instead of a rope.'

They testified, detailing for the marshal and Jim things Stark had hired them to do, blaming him for all the scare tactics used to force other ranchers into signing away their land, and even the murder of the bar-girl Stark had pawned off on Stroud. Jim knew they would testify against Dubias Phinney and bet the lawyer would name names of higher-ups to avoid hanging.

A noose was already slung over a branch. Jim went to the back of the house to fetch his bay and mounted. When he rode around front again the marshal's men had carted off the cowhands and a few were searching the house.

The marshal smiled at Jim with satisfaction. 'He made a hell of a tree ornament . . . '

Jim felt a grim sense of completion and gigged his horse into a steady ground-eating pace.

When he reached the ranch, Ruby was waiting for him on the porch and he reckoned this time there was no fork in the trail.

Only the straight and narrow.

THE END

We do hope that you have enjoyed reading this large print book.

Did you know that all of our titles are available for purchase?

We publish a wide range of high quality large print books including:
Romances, Mysteries, Classics
General Fiction
Non Fiction and Westerns

Special interest titles available in large print are:
The Little Oxford Dictionary
Music Book, Song Book
Hymn Book, Service Book

Also available from us courtesy of Oxford University Press:
Young Readers' Dictionary
(large print edition)
Young Readers' Thesaurus
(large print edition)

For further information or a free brochure, please contact us at:
Ulverscroft Large Print Books Ltd.,
The Green, Bradgate Road, Anstey,
Leicester, LE7 7FU, England.
Tel: (00 44) **0116 236 4325**
Fax: (00 44) **0116 234 0205**

Other titles in the
Linford Western Library:

THE CHISELLER

Tex Larrigan

Soon the paddle-steamer would be on its long journey down the Missouri River to St Louis. Now, all Saul Rhymer had to do was to play the last master-stroke of the evening. He looked at the mounting pile of gold and dollar bills and again at the cards in his hand. Then, looking around the table, he produced the deed to the goldmine in Montana. 'Let's play poker!' But little did he know how that journey back to St Louis would change his life so drastically.